A NEW CAMPER SPELLS TROUBLE

KATIE was the first to suggest a "Welcome" banner for the new girl assigned to Cabin Six . . . but that was before they met her.

SARAH was determined to uncover some good in their new bunkmate . . . and that was going to be difficult.

TRINA agreed to go along with Sarah's plan to bombard the newcomer with friendliness . . . and hope for the best.

MEGAN, with her usual vivid imagination, was convinced the new girl was put in Cabin Six just to test them.

ERIN didn't want to share her space with anyone . . . least of all this one.

MARILYN KAYE is the author of many popular books for young readers, including the "Out of This World" series and the "Sisters" books. She is an associate professor at St. John's University and lives in Brooklyn, New York.

Camp Sunnyside is the camp Marilyn Kaye wishes that she had gone to every summer when she was a kid.

New Girl in Cabin Six

Marilyn Kaye

AN AVON  CAMELOT BOOK

CAMP SUNNYSIDE FRIENDS #4: NEW GIRL IN CABIN SIX is an
original publication of Avon Books. This work has never before appeared in book form.

AVON BOOKS
A division of
The Hearst Corporation
105 Madison Avenue
New York, New York 10016

Copyright © 1989 by Marilyn Kaye
Published by arrangement with the author
Library of Congress Catalog Card Number: 89-91301
ISBN: 0-380-75703-6
RL: 5.0

First Avon Camelot Printing: November 1989

CAMELOT TRADEMARK REG. U.S. PAT. OFF. AND IN OTHER COUNTRIES, MARCA
REGISTRADA, HECHO EN U.S.A.

Printed in the U.S.A.

OPM 10 9 8 7 6 5 4 3 2 1

For Melissa Osborn

New Girl in Cabin Six

Chapter 1

Sarah Fine lay on her top bunk, her head propped up with pillows, her knees bent, and her open book resting comfortably on her stomach. Rest period was her favorite time of day at Camp Sunnyside. It was her one time to read in absolute peace and quiet.

Of course, she read at other times too—during the free period, at night under her blanket with a flashlight, and whenever she came up with an excuse to get out of another camp activity.

But rest period was best. She didn't have to make up excuses or hide from their counselor, Carolyn, or listen to her friends in cabin six urge her to join them in some game. During rest period, they were supposed to be quiet. In fact, they were even encouraged to take a nap.

But no self-respecting eleven year old took a

nap. Peering over her book, Sarah checked to see what her cabin mates were doing.

Trina Sandburg was sitting cross-legged on her bed, writing a letter. Above her, Katie Dillon wore headphones attached to a cassette player. She was tapping her feet to the music no one else could hear and thumbing through a comic book. Over in the corner, on the single bed, Erin Chapman was painting her fingernails.

Sarah didn't have to look beneath her own bunk to know what Megan Lindsay was doing. She knew from experience that Megan would be lying there with her eyes closed—not sleeping, only daydreaming.

Nothing was out of the ordinary. All the girls were doing what they always did during rest period. The cabin six gang had been together at Camp Sunnyside for three years, and Sarah knew them all so well she was hardly ever surprised by anything they said or did. Each of them was different, but somehow they managed to get along with one another—well, most of the time.

Sarah went back to her book. It was a pretty big fat book, longer than the ones she usually read. She wished she could stay there all day, just reading. It wasn't that she hated the camp activities. She wasn't too crazy about volleyball or softball, but swimming was okay, and archery was so-so. Camp fires were fun, too. And she really liked being with her friends.

But next to that, what she liked best of all was reading. And there never seemed to be enough time for that.

Suddenly, without warning, Katie pulled the headphones off her head. "Darn! My batteries are dead!"

Sarah glanced at her reprovingly. "Katie! Shh!" No talking during rest period was a rule.

But Katie was never one for following rules. "That's dumb," she muttered. For a second, she stared down at her comic book. Then she picked it up and flung it across the room.

"Hey!" Erin yelled. "You almost knocked over my polish!"

"Sorry. But I'm bored!"

Sarah shook her head in amusement. Maybe she loved rest periods, but she knew very well that Katie hated them. She didn't like to have to be still and quiet.

Katie climbed down from her bunk and began to pace the room. "How much longer do we have to sit around like this?" she asked no one in particular.

Trina checked her watch and replied in a

whisper. "Just five more minutes. Katie, *please* keep your voice down. If Carolyn hears you, we'll get a demerit."

Trina's warning worked. Katie glanced at the closed door leading to their counselor's room and lowered her voice. "Okay, okay." She retrieved her comic book and climbed back up to her bed.

Only five more minutes, Sarah thought sadly. And she was just getting to an exciting part! Maybe she could carry the book with her to arts and crafts. But she doubted she'd get away with it. The arts and crafts counselor had eyes like a hawk. And reading just wasn't considered an artistic activity.

To her, it didn't seem like five minutes, but more like five seconds when the tall, fair-haired counselor opened her door and came into the cabin. "Rest period's over," Carolyn announced, and Katie responded with a cry of joy.

The cabin came alive. Rapidly, Katie grabbed her tennis shoes and put them on. Trina folded her letter and put it aside. Erin put the cap on her polish bottle and started waving her hands in the air to dry.

Reluctantly, Sarah inserted a bookmark into her book, and with one last longing look at it climbed down from her bunk.

Only Megan hadn't stirred. Sarah snapped

her fingers in the redhead's face, and her bunk mate opened her eyes.

"And where have you been?" Sarah asked in a teasing voice.

Megan smiled dreamily. "Wimbledon. Center court."

Sarah grinned. If reading was *her* passion, tennis was Megan's. Just about the only time Megan didn't daydream was while she was playing tennis.

Carolyn checked the schedule on the bulletin board. "Time for arts and crafts," she said.

"But my nails aren't dry yet," Erin objected as she flapped her hands wildly.

"They'll dry on the way," Carolyn replied. "C'mon, girls, you know Donna doesn't like you to be late."

For a second, Sarah debated climbing back up the ladder and grabbing her book. But Carolyn was watching them all, and the counselor knew Sarah too well to allow her to head for arts and crafts with a book in her hand.

Oh well, she thought, at least it was arts and crafts and not one of those athletic activities. She joined her cabin mates, who were already leaving the cabin.

"I'm reading the best book," she told the others as they made their way over to the arts and crafts cabin.

Katie looked at her in alarm. "It's not a romance, is it?"

The others were looking at her suspiciously too, and Sarah knew why. The cabin six girls had gotten themselves into some trouble before because of Sarah's romance novels. She'd lent some to Megan, who had used them as guidelines in a cabin effort to play Cupid between their counselor and the camp handyman, Teddy. They'd been seeing each other, but then they broke up, and the girls had wanted to get them back together. But Megan's wild imagination and their efforts had backfired—and almost resulted in Carolyn's getting fired!

"No, it's not a romance," Sarah assured Katie. "It's a mystery."

"What's it about?" Megan asked. The others looked interested too. Even though they weren't great readers like Sarah, they enjoyed listening to her describe the books she was always reading.

"Well, there are six people who are all visiting this old uncle of theirs who nobody likes because he's mean and cranky. But he's also very rich. Anyway, they get snowbound there, and they can't leave. Then, the old man gets real sick, and it looks like someone's trying to poison him for his money. Only nobody knows who did it. It's really exciting, and I can't wait to find out which one is the villain."

"Can you guess who did it?" Trina asked.

"No. One of the suspects is a gambler, and he's always talking about how he wishes he had more money. So you're supposed to think he did it. But you know how mysteries are. The person who acts like the bad guy is never the real villain."

"That's why I don't like mystery books," Katie stated. "They're not realistic at all. In real life, you can tell who's really good and who's really bad." She dropped her voice to a whisper as they neared another group of girls. "Think about Maura."

Sarah looked at the cabin nine girls who were just ahead of them. Maura Kingsley, the snottiest girl at Camp Sunnyside, was with them.

"Oh, you're always picking on Maura," Erin said. "I think she's neat."

Sarah had to agree with Katie. Maura acted terribly stuck-up, and she really wasn't a nice person. When she was captain of her color war team, Maura had played a lot of nasty tricks on the other team. And when Sarah was just learning to swim, Maura had poked fun at her.

7

"What are we doing in arts and crafts today?" Megan asked as they arrived at the cabin.

"We're supposed to be starting something new," Trina remarked.

"Do you know what it is?" Sarah asked her.

"No, Donna didn't say."

"I hope we're not going to be working with clay," Erin said worriedly, eyeing her freshly painted nails.

But there was no sign of clay on the tables in the arts and crafts cabin. There were only big pads of plain white paper and colored marking pens. On the counselor's desk, there was a huge stack of plain white sweatshirts.

The cabin six girls took their places at one of the tables and gave their attention to the arts and crafts counselor. "This week," Donna announced, "you're all going to have the opportunity to be fashion designers!"

Sarah watched Erin's face brighten. Erin was seriously into fashion.

"Each of you is going to design your own sweatshirt," Donna continued. "For the next couple of days, you can sketch and color some ideas on these pads. Then, when you've come up with a design you really like, you'll each get a sweatshirt and create your design right on the fabric."

8

General sounds of approval rose from the group. Even Sarah had to admit this sounded like fun—even if she didn't have the slightest idea what kind of sweatshirt she'd like to make. She just wasn't creative that way. But Donna was always good at helping them come up with ideas.

"Can we use sequins?" Erin asked.

Donna nodded. "And paints and ribbons and buttons. But you need to carefully plan your design before you even think about attacking a sweatshirt. There's only one for each of you, so you don't want to make any big mistakes. Now, I want you all to look at a blank sheet of paper and imagine it as the front of a sweatshirt. You can use as much paper as you want."

The room fell silent. Some girls just stared at their paper with looks of concentration on their faces. Others picked up markers and began drawing.

Sarah looked down at the pad. But instead of thinking about a sweatshirt, her mind wandered back to her book. Who was the villain? Who was the least likely person to poison the old man? She considered the characters. The glamorous movie star? The timid secretary? There were so many possibilities. . . .

"Do you have any bright ideas, Sarah?"

9

For one confused moment, Sarah thought Donna was referring to the mystery. Then she realized Donna was talking about the sweatshirt.

"Not really," she confessed. She looked around to see what her friends were drawing. Trina had covered a sheet with big daisies, and she was studying them thoughtfully. Erin was drawing hearts. Megan's page had two odd-looking shapes that reminded Sarah of frying pans.

"Megan, what are those supposed to be?" Donna asked.

"Tennis rackets." Megan made a face. "I guess I'm not much of an artist."

Donna laughed. "Let me see if I can help."

As she moved over to work with Megan, Sarah contemplated her own blank page. What kind of design could she come up with? Like Megan, she wasn't an artist either.

But maybe she didn't have to do a picture. Maybe her sweatshirt could just have words. That was something she knew she was good at. In fact, she knew that someday she would be a writer.

But what could she write on a sweatshirt? A poem, maybe? Or a slogan—something clever and funny.

Suddenly, she had an idea. She selected a red marking pen. Then, very carefully, she wrote the word "mystery" on the top of the sheet. Next to it, she put a question mark.

Then she took a blue pen, and under "mystery," she wrote "romance." What would be a good symbol for a romance book? Of course—a heart!

Now, what other kinds of books did she like? There was science fiction. But what could she draw as a symbol for it? Some sort of alien creature, maybe.

"How does this look?" Katie asked. She held up a sheet of paper.

"That's neat!" Sarah exclaimed. Katie had covered her paper with stars and moons and planets.

"I think I'll paint the background blue," Katie said, "and use silver for all the stars and stuff. Then it would look like the night sky."

"But the sky has only one moon," Trina pointed out gently. "You've got three—no, four moons."

Katie frowned. "Oh yeah, you're right."

"But that's just on earth," Donna said. "Maybe this is the night sky from another planet."

Katie grinned. "Yeah! Like, maybe this is what an extraterrestrial would see at night!"

"Speaking of extraterrestrials," Sarah said, "does anyone know how to draw one?"

But before anyone could answer her, the door to the cabin opened and Carolyn hurried in. Sarah watched curiously as their counselor had a whispered conversation with Donna.

"Right now?" she heard Donna ask. Carolyn nodded. Then she came over to their table.

"Girls, I hate to cut this short," she said, "but Ms. Winkle wants to see you."

The girls exchanged startled looks. "What for?" Katie asked.

"I don't know," Carolyn said. "But put away your stuff and let's go."

Sarah bit her lower lip. Why would the camp director want to see them? Had they gathered *that* many demerits already? Had one of them done something the others didn't know about?

She saw the same worried looks on all the faces. "Did we do something wrong?" Trina asked.

"Not that I know of," Carolyn said. "I just got this note, saying she wants to see you all in her office right now. And me too."

Everyone seemed just as puzzled as Sarah was. Certainly, cabin six had been involved in

12

some mischievous activities this summer. The last time they had all been in Ms. Winkle's office was when they confessed to their disastrous matchmaking attempt. But they hadn't done anything really crazy lately. Not that Sarah could think of.

"You can work more on your drawings tomorrow," Donna said.

"What do you think this is all about?" Megan asked Sarah as they recapped their markers. Quickly, the girls gathered their pads and piled them together.

"I haven't the slightest idea," Sarah said. Her stomach was jumping nervously as the girls followed Carolyn out of the cabin. "But I guess we're about to find out."

Chapter 2

The group was unusually quiet as they crossed the campgrounds with Carolyn in the lead.

"Do you think we're going to be sent home?" Megan whispered to Sarah.

"Don't be silly," Sarah whispered back. "We haven't done anything to be sent home for." She paused. "Have we?"

"I don't *think* so," Megan murmured, but she still looked nervous. They all did. Occasionally, one of the girls would glance quickly at another and then just as quickly avert her eyes. Sarah wondered if they were all thinking what she was thinking—that one of them had committed some awful act that was now getting the whole cabin in trouble.

But even though she was thinking about that, she had a hard time believing that was actually the case. The cabin six girls were together so much, it wouldn't be easy for one of them to be involved in something the others knew nothing about.

And surely they couldn't have collected so many demerits that Ms. Winkle would be calling them to her office. Oh, they got the ordinary occasional demerit for a dirty tee shirt or not having lights out on time. But lately cabin six had been doing really well. Why, just last week, they had received the weekly award for neatest cabin. Ms. Winkle herself had presented them with the certificate. What could possibly be wrong? Sarah couldn't think of anything.

But even so, as they entered the main building, Sarah could feel her heart beating. "Go right in," the secretary told them, cocking her head toward Ms. Winkle's office. As they went in, Sarah stared at the floor, fearful of seeing the expression on the camp director's face. But when she finally raised her head, she found she was in for a big surprise.

Ms. Winkle was smiling at them. As usual, she looked a little flustered and harried but definitely not angry. "Hello, girls. Have a seat."

The girls, still eyeing her apprehensively, positioned themselves on the couch and chairs that surrounded Ms. Winkle's desk.

16

"I have a special favor to ask of you," Ms. Winkle told them. "But before I tell you what the favor is, I want to tell you why I'm choosing your cabin."

Everyone looked puzzled, and Sarah tried not to smile. It was so typical of Ms. Winkle to talk in a roundabout way before getting to the point.

"You cabin six girls are all old-timers," Ms. Winkle continued. "And I know you've got the real Sunnyside spirit. You're friendly and cheerful, and you're not involved in petty snobbery." As she went on, her voice became dreamy. "You're the kind of girls who don't judge others by outward appearances. You look for the inner qualities of a person."

By now, they were all looking at the camp director in bewilderment. What was she talking about, Sarah wondered. Ms. Winkle certainly didn't know them as individuals all that well. And Sarah couldn't help sneaking a peek to see Erin's reaction to all this praise. Because Erin was *not* big on inner qualities. She was likely to be much more impressed with the quality of someone's clothes!

"And that's why I'm asking cabin six to do me this favor," Ms. Winkle finished. And she looked at them expectantly. "How do you feel about it?"

17

Carolyn coughed. "Um, what's the favor, Ms. Winkle?"

The camp director's eyes widened, and then she laughed. "Oh, of course, I haven't told you! I'm asking if you girls would accept a new camper in your cabin."

Five mouths fell open. Sarah could tell they were all thinking the same thing. A new camper? In cabin six? In the middle of the summer? It was true that some of the younger campers came only for short sessions. But girls their age always came for the entire summer.

Ms. Winkle responded to their unasked questions. "The girl I'm talking about is my niece, Jackie. She's going to be visiting here for a week. Of course, she could stay with me, but she's never been to a summer camp before, and I'd rather she have a real Sunnyside experience. And she can have that only in a cabin with real Sunnyside girls."

As the girls were still absorbing this startling announcement, Carolyn spoke up. "We'll be glad to have your niece with us, Ms. Winkle. And I know my girls will do everything to make her feel welcome. How about it, girls?"

Trina nodded. "It'll be fun having her. And we'll show her around and introduce her to everyone."

18

"Yeah," Katie agreed. "And we'll make sure she has a good time. You've definitely picked the right cabin, Ms. Winkle. How old is Jackie?"

"Eleven," Ms. Winkle said. "Just like all of you."

Erin tossed her head. "I'm almost twelve," she murmured, but no one paid any attention.

"We'll take good care of her," Sarah said.

"Does she play tennis?" Megan asked eagerly.

"I'm not sure," Ms. Winkle said vaguely. "To tell you the truth, I haven't seen her for some time. Anyway, I'm gratified that you're all being so good about this. But I'm not surprised, because you're Sunnyside girls!"

They basked in the warmth of her praise, although Sarah couldn't help wondering what Ms. Winkle would think if she knew what some of the Sunnyside girls—like Maura—were really like.

Erin spoke for the first time. And she didn't sound terribly enthusiastic. "When is she coming?"

"Tomorrow," Ms. Winkle said. "Now, why don't you all run along to dinner. Carolyn, could you stay a moment? I'd like to talk with you privately."

The girls left quietly, but once outside they all started talking at once.

"I didn't know Ms. Winkle thought we were so special," Megan said. "She must really like us a lot to put her niece in our cabin."

Katie laughed. "I don't think that's why she picked us. There are three cabins of eleven year olds, and the other two have six girls. We've got only five. It makes sense for her to put Jackie with us."

"I wonder what she's like?" Sarah pondered.

"I hope she's not snotty," Megan said. "I mean, being the camp director's niece and all."

"We'll really have to be very, very nice to her," Trina said.

"No kidding," Katie remarked. "If we're not, she might go running to Ms. Winkle and complain about us."

Trina looked at Katie reprovingly. "That's not what I meant."

Sarah knew what Trina was saying. "She'll probably feel strange, being new and not knowing anyone. We have to make an extra special effort to include her in everything."

"What *I* want to know," Erin said, "is where she's going to sleep."

"In our cabin," Megan replied. "Weren't you listening?"

Erin gazed at her in disdain. "I know she's going to be in our cabin, dummy. What I mean is, where are they going to put her bed?"

"Maybe they'll squeeze a cot into the corner," Katie suggested.

Erin shook her head. "There's not enough room."

They were nearing the dining hall, and everyone's steps quickened. But then Sarah saw something out of the corner of her eye that distracted her and made her stop.

It was a girl, sitting alone under a tree at the far end of the dining hall. Sarah pushed her glasses up from where they had fallen to the tip of her nose and peered at her.

Sarah didn't recognize her, but all she could see was that the girl had stringy light brown hair. She couldn't figure out her size, shape, or age because she was huddled over and her knees were drawn up to her chest. And her face was buried in her hands.

Trina had noticed her too and paused as the others moved on. "Who's that?"

"I don't know," Sarah said. "But I think maybe she's crying."

"Is she hurt?" Trina wondered.

"C'mon, you guys," Katie called.

"We'll be there in a second," Sarah yelled

21

back. Then she turned to Trina. "Maybe we should go see if something's wrong with her."

Trina agreed, and they made their way over to the forlorn girl. "Are you okay?" Sarah asked her.

The girl raised her head. Now that she could see her, Sarah realized she was younger—maybe eight or nine—small, and thin. And she could also see that she'd definitely been crying. Her face was puffy, her cheeks were wet, and her eyes were red.

"What's wrong?" Trina asked gently.

The girl mumbled something, and Sarah could barely hear her, but she caught the word "home." And she recognized the symptoms. "Are you homesick?"

The girl nodded, and fresh tears began to pour from her eyes.

"You must be one of the new girls," Sarah said.

"I just came last week," the girl said, sniffling. "And I want to go home."

Sarah and Trina exchanged meaningful looks. It seemed like ages ago, but Sarah could remember being a little homesick the very first time she came to Sunnyside. They'd all felt that way, and more than one cabin six girl had shed a few tears during the first week at camp.

"We understand," Trina said. "It's hard at first, being away from home. But you'll make friends, and you'll have a wonderful time here."

"I want to go home," the girl repeated.

A counselor approached them. "Beth! There you are! I've been looking everywhere for you."

Beth looked at the counselor as if she were a guard coming to escort her back to prison. The counselor sighed. It was obvious she knew about Beth's problem. "C'mon, honey, you'll feel better after dinner."

The prospect of food didn't appear to do much to improve Beth's attitude. But she got up and accepted the counselor's offer of a handkerchief.

"We were just telling her she'll stop feeling homesick soon," Trina said, and the counselor smiled gratefully.

"I'm sure Beth's going to love Sunnyside once she gets used to it," she said brightly, putting an arm around her.

But as she watched them walk toward the dining hall, Sarah had doubts. "That's the worst case of homesickness I've ever seen."

"I hope Jackie doesn't get homesick like that," Trina worried.

"We won't let her," Sarah stated. "We'll just keep her busy, and she'll have no time to think about home. Hey, I'm starving."

23

"Me too," Trina agreed, and they hurried into the dining hall. They picked up their dinner trays and joined the others at their table.

A few minutes later, Carolyn appeared. "You guys were really terrific in Ms. Winkle's office," she said. "She feels good about putting her niece in with you."

"Where's she going to sleep?" Erin demanded.

But Carolyn didn't hear her. She seemed to have something else on her mind. "Ms. Winkle told me more about Jackie, and we decided there's something else you should know about her. You see, her parents are getting divorced, and that's why Jackie's coming here for a week. Her parents felt it best that she be away while her father is moving out of their house."

The girls contemplated this new information. Trina, in particular, looked very sympathetic, and Sarah remembered that her parents had gotten divorced over the winter.

"I know how she must be feeling," Trina said softly. "It's pretty rough at the beginning."

"She'll really need friends," Katie said. "She might want to talk about it all."

"Or she just might want people to help her forget abut it," Megan said.

Sarah envisioned a sad, forlorn girl, sort of

24

like the one they'd just seen—only not crying so much, she hoped. But in any case, she felt a strong surge of protective warmth toward Ms. Winkle's niece. "We'll do everything we can to make her feel good," she said.

Carolyn beamed at them. "I knew I could count on all of you to be understanding."

Four heads bobbed up and down. Only one of them wasn't nodding or looking too understanding either. "Where is she going to sleep?" Erin asked again.

Carolyn's smile faded slightly. "Well, I was going to talk to you especially about that, Erin."

Erin's eyes narrowed. "Why?"

"There's no room in the cabin for another single bed. So we'll need to turn your single bed into a bunk bed for you and Jackie to share."

Erin was appalled. "I can't sleep in a bunk bed!"

"Why not?" Carolyn asked.

The other girls looked at one another knowingly. But they let Erin explain to Carolyn.

"My parents pay extra so I can have my own single bed."

"But it's just for a week," Carolyn said. "And you can have your choice of bottom or top."

"But if I'm on top I get dizzy," Erin protested.

25

"And if I'm on the bottom, I feel—what's that word that means all closed in?"

"Claustrophobic," Sarah supplied.

"Yeah, that's it. Anyway, that's why my parents arranged for me to have my own bed when I first came here. And I've had it for three years now."

Carolyn nodded slowly. "And you haven't tried a bunk bed in three years?"

Erin shook her head, and Carolyn eyed her thoughtfully.

"Then you really don't know if you'll still feel dizzy or claustrophobic. You were only nine when you first came here. And you're almost twelve now. You've probably grown out of those childish feelings."

She was smart to use the word "childish," Sarah thought. If there was one word Erin would never want to be associated with, it was "childish."

Erin hesitated, and Carolyn smiled brightly. "Erin, I was counting on you to make this small sacrifice for a week. I know some girls might make a fuss, but you're mature enough to handle it."

Sarah grinned at Katie, and Katie winked back. They all knew that "mature" was another magic word with Erin. She always acted like

26

she was much more sophisticated than the others.

Erin still didn't look thrilled with the prospect. But she nodded grudgingly. "Okay. As long as it's only for one week."

Carolyn smiled in relief. And Sarah was glad that Erin wasn't going to go on and on arguing about the bed. But there was a little worry in the back of her mind.

Erin might have agreed to the bunk bed, but she still wasn't pleased about this arrangement. And that meant she might have a grudge against Jackie right off.

Oh well, she thought as she dug into her plate of spaghetti, she wasn't going to worry about Erin being unfriendly. She and the others would just have to be twice as nice to make up for her.

Chapter 3

Sarah had planned to get back to her mystery book during free period the next day, but Katie had other plans for the group. She and Megan came into the cabin dragging a long length of brown wrapping paper.

Sarah put her book aside. "What's that?"

"We got it from Donna," Katie explained. "We're going to make a Welcome Jackie banner and hang it on the front of the cabin."

"That's a great idea," Sarah said, scrambling down her ladder.

Trina agreed. "This way she'll know we want her here, even before she walks in."

Only Erin seemed to have doubts. "Personally, if I saw my name on a banner like that, I'd be embarrassed."

"Oh, you would not," Katie chided her.

"You'd be thrilled." She lay the paper down on the floor. "Who's good at lettering?"

"I'll do it," Trina offered. "I'll outline in pencil, and then we can fill in the letters with marking pens." She knelt down on the floor and got to work.

"I had an idea, too," Megan said. "At the camp fire tonight, we can introduce her to the whole camp, and sing that welcome to Sunnyside song, like we did for the new campers who came last week."

Now it was Sarah's turn to have some doubts. "You know, maybe we should wait and see what she's like. If she's the shy type, that might be too much."

"But Ms. Winkle would love it," Katie said. "When she sees how nice we are to her niece, she'll think we're great. And we'll be able to get away with murder this summer!"

"Katie!" Trina exclaimed.

Katie laughed. "Okay, I'm sorry. I really do want to make Jackie feel welcome. But it won't hurt us to get on Ms. Winkle's good side too!"

By now, they were all on the floor with marking pens, filling in Trina's neatly outlined letters. Erin just stood there, hands on her hips, shaking her head. "I hope this girl appreciates all the effort we're making for her."

30

Sarah eyed her skeptically. "I don't see *you* making much of an effort."

Erin sniffed. *"I'm* making the biggest sacrifice of all." As if on cue, the cabin door opened, and in came Teddy, the handyman, with his assistant. Between them, they were carrying a bed and posters. Following them was Carolyn with an armful of sheets and towels.

"Here's the top half of your bed," Teddy announced cheerfully.

Erin glared at him. Then, with a huge, resigned sigh, she stepped away from her single bed and allowed them to get to work.

"We all appreciate this so much," Carolyn murmured soothingly to Erin.

Sarah glanced at Megan and rolled her eyes. Everyone was acting like Erin was doing something wonderful for Jackie. Well, it was worth it if it kept Erin from being snotty to the new girl. "Do you know what time she's coming?" she asked the counselor.

Carolyn checked her watch. "Any minute now. What are you guys doing, anyway?"

Sarah concentrated on rapidly filling in letters while Katie explained. "We're making this banner, and we're thinking about singing her the welcome song tonight at the camp fire."

"Do you think we should plan any special activities?" Trina asked.

"I asked cabin seven to have a softball game with us Friday," Katie announced.

"Softball, yuck," Sarah growled. It had to be her least favorite activity. But hastily, she added, "That'll be nice for Jackie. I'll even pretend I'm having fun." She filled in the dot at the top of the "i" in "Jackie," and then stood up. "Hey, this looks good. We better put it up right away before she gets here."

"Erin, get the tape," Katie ordered. The others grabbed the four corners of the banner and carried it outside. Being the tallest, Trina fixed the top of the banner to the wall, while the others taped the bottom.

"Oh, how lovely!" At the sound of Ms. Winkle's voice, the girls turned. "What a nice sign!"

Normally, Sarah would have responded with an immediate "thank you." But like the others, she was too busy staring at the girl who stood by Ms. Winkle's side to remember her manners.

She was average height and size, but that was about all you could call average about her. Her hair was black and short, and she must have used tons of gook on it because it stuck up in the air. She wore a black tee shirt, black jeans, and an expression that suggested she was in a black mood.

Ms. Winkle seemed even more flustered than usual. "Girls, this is my niece, Jackie. Jackie, this is . . ." she hesitated, and Sarah grinned. Ms. Winkle was famous for never remembering names.

"We'll introduce ourselves," Sarah said quickly, and Ms. Winkle smiled in gratitude. "Good! I'll just run inside and have a word with your counselor." She disappeared into the cabin.

There was a moment of silence, and then Katie spoke. "Welcome to Sunnyside!"

She might as well have been speaking a foreign language. Jackie didn't respond at all.

"Um, I'm Katie. This is Trina, Sarah, Megan, and Erin."

"Hi," they chorused. But Jackie still didn't say anything. She sauntered past them, ignoring the banner, and examined the cabin, peeking inside a window. Then she said her first words. "This looks like a real dump."

Sarah couldn't believe her ears. Was Jackie making a joke? She laughed uncertainly. "Yeah, well, it's not the Taj Mahal, that's for sure."

"But we like it," Katie stated.

Jackie uttered a short, harsh laugh. "Yeah. That figures."

33

The others looked at each other in bewilderment. What was that supposed to mean? "Where are you from?" Sarah asked Jackie.

"New York."

"Oh, how lucky you are!" Trina said. "I've only been to New York once, but I loved it. There are so many wonderful museums, and all those theaters."

Jackie shrugged. "I don't know about that stuff. I just hang out with my gang."

"Your—your gang?" Megan asked faintly.

"Yeah. We're called the Sharkettes."

Erin was looking at Jackie as if she were some sort of creature from outer space. "What does your gang do?"

Jackie just shrugged again. "Not much. We just hang around."

"We've got lots to do here," Katie told her. "Swimming and horses—"

"And tennis," Megan added.

Jackie didn't look impressed. Maybe she's not the athletic type either, Sarah thought. "If you like to read, I've got lots of books you can borrow," she offered.

Jackie gave that odd laugh again. It sounded more like she was snorting. "Read! I never read. I got better things to do with my time."

"Like what?" Trina asked.

Now Jackie smiled, but it wasn't a nice, friendly sort of smile. It was more like she had some mysterious secret. "That's my business, not yours." Then she yawned, right in their faces. "I'm going inside to lie down." She started toward the door.

"You have the top bunk," Erin called after her anxiously. But Jackie didn't even acknowledge that she'd heard her, and let the door of the cabin slam behind her.

There was a total silence among the group. It was as if they were all in a state of shock. Finally, Katie, in a typically blunt way, said what they were all thinking. "She's awful."

"I don't think she wants to be here," Megan said in a small voice.

"She looks like a juvenile delinquent," Erin stated. "Are we really going to let someone like that stay in our cabin?"

Trina's face was troubled. "I guess she's not what we expected."

"That's putting it mildly," Erin snapped.

Sarah didn't say anything at first. She was thinking.

The cabin door opened. Teddy and the other handyman came out, followed by Carolyn and Ms. Winkle. Sarah examined their faces. They all looked a little uneasy.

"Thanks for fixing the bed," Carolyn said.

"No problem," Teddy replied. He saluted the campers. "Have fun with your new cabin mate," he called to them. Sarah could have sworn she detected a twinkle in his eye.

Ms. Winkle was wringing her hands as she spoke to Carolyn. Her voice was soft, but Sarah caught the tail end of her words. "And let me know if you have any problems." Then she hurried off.

Carolyn joined the girls. "Did you girls have a chance to talk with Jackie?"

They avoided her eyes as they nodded, and no one made a comment. But Carolyn was watching them intently. "And what do you think of her?"

"She's—kind of tough, isn't she?" Katie said.

"I hate the way she looks," Erin muttered.

"Well, don't make snap judgments based on appearances," Carolyn said. "I'm sure there's more to Jackie than meets the eye. Just give her time."

"How much?" Katie asked.

"How much what?"

"How much time do we need to give her?"

Carolyn shook her head in exasperation. "As much time as it takes, Katie."

Katie made a face, but she nodded. "Okay.

But I hope she's acting normal by camp fire time. Otherwise, *I'm* not singing a welcome song to her."

Even Sarah had to admit she wouldn't feel very sincere singing "We're happy to have you here" to Jackie either.

The fire was burning brightly, sending sparks into the night sky. Some campers were toasting marshmallows, while others were tossing a disk that glowed in the dark. In a few minutes, they'd all gather around the fire and start singing.

"Well?" Megan asked. "Are we going to sing her the welcome song?"

"I'm not singing to her," Erin stated flatly. Sarah couldn't tell if the red in Erin's face was a reflection of the flames or if it was just pure anger. "I can't believe she took the bottom bunk, when I *told* her to take the top one."

"Well, at least now you won't get claustrophobic," Sarah said lightly. But trying to sound cheerful took a real effort. Jackie had been at Sunnyside for half a day, and she was still behaving the way she had when she arrived. She'd barely spoken to them at all unless they asked her a direct question. And then she only replied with one or two sullen words.

"I think we should just ignore her and pretend she's not here," Katie said.

"We don't have to pretend," Megan said, looking around. "Where is she, anyway?"

"I don't know and I don't care," Erin said.

Sarah got up. "I'm going to look for her. Anyone want to come with me?"

"I will." Trina stood up, and together they walked away from the crowd. "Sarah, why do you think Jackie's so unfriendly?"

"I don't know," Sarah said. "I've been thinking about her. Maybe she's not like that at all. Maybe she's just putting on a big act."

"But why would she do that?"

"I don't know," Sarah said again. "It's just an idea. Hey, is that her over there?" Her glasses had slipped down her nose, and she squinted at a solitary figure sitting on a rock.

"No, it's that girl we talked to yesterday. The one who was so homesick."

"Hi, Beth," Sarah called. The younger girl looked up. Sarah and Trina went over to her.

"Are you feeling better?" Trina asked.

Beth shook her head. "I'm going to the infirmary," she said in a voice that was barely audible.

"You mean, you're actually sick?" Sarah asked.

38

"No. But I'm going to say I feel sick. And then maybe they'll call my parents and tell them to take me home."

"Oh, Beth," Trina said, "why don't you give Sunnyside a chance? Honestly, you won't be homesick for long."

Again, Beth shook her head. Then she got off the rock and walked away.

"Poor kid," Sarah said. Then she wrinkled her nose. "Do you smell something funny?"

Trina sniffed. Then she nodded. "Yeah. It's coming from over there."

The girls made their way around a clump of bushes. And then they both gasped. Jackie was sitting alone on the ground. And she was smoking a cigarette.

"Jackie!" Trina exclaimed in horror. "What are you doing?"

Jackie didn't make any attempt to hide the cigarette. "What does it look like?" she asked snidely. Then she inhaled and blew a stream of smoke right into Trina's face. Trina started coughing.

Sarah gazed at the girl evenly. "Put that out." She was surprised at how authoritative she sounded. But Jackie wasn't impressed.

"Why should I?"

"Because it's disgusting," Sarah said. "Not to

39

mention the fact that smoking is against the rules. You could get sent home for that. Even if you are Ms. Winkle's niece."

Jackie sneered at them. "Maybe I want to get sent home. I'd have a better time there than I'm having here."

"You haven't even been here a full day yet!" Trina protested. "How do you know you can't have a good time here?"

"I can tell." Jackie tossed the cigarette on the ground. Sarah stepped on it and ground it out. Then she looked at Jackie thoughtfully. "What would you be doing at home right now?"

"Hanging out with my gang," Jackie replied.

"But what do you do when you're hanging out?" Trina asked.

"Oh, lots of things. Sometimes we go in a drugstore and swipe stuff."

"You—you shoplift?" Sarah asked in disbelief.

"Sure. It's no big deal." Jackie got up. "I'm going back to the cabin."

"You're not supposed to go back by yourself," Trina said. "That's a rule."

"You got a lot of stupid rules here," Jackie said. "That doesn't mean I have to obey them."

"Come back to the camp fire," Trina pleaded. "We're going to start singing."

"Oh, goody-goody," Jackie said sarcastically.

"There you girls are!" Carolyn emerged from the bushes. "Jackie, your aunt is looking for you." She placed an arm lightly around Jackie's shoulders and started leading her back toward the camp fire. Jackie didn't look too pleased, but at least she didn't pull away.

Trina and Sarah followed a few yards behind. "Do you believe what she said?" Trina asked. "About stealing things?"

"I don't know," Sarah said. "Maybe she was just trying to shock us. Like with the cigarette. I don't know anyone who smokes, but the way she was holding it didn't look very natural to me. And she must have known someone would come looking for her. I'll bet she doesn't really smoke. And that story about shoplifting might have been a big fat lie."

Trina thought about this. "Do you think we should tell Carolyn?"

"No," Sarah said firmly. "I think we should be extra nice to Jackie and try to get to know her better. Like Carolyn said, we shouldn't judge her right away. And remember what Ms. Winkle said about inner qualities? Maybe, deep inside, Jackie's really a good person."

Trina nodded. "Okay. Let's not tell the others about the cigarette or the shoplifting. And we have to get them to be nice to her no matter how she acts."

"Okay." But Sarah wasn't so sure how likely they were to convince the others to follow along. Megan might—but she had a feeling Erin and Katie had pretty much made up their minds about Jackie.

But Sarah hadn't. She was determined to find out if there was something under Jackie's tough exterior. She wanted to find the real Jackie.

She only hoped the real Jackie would be better than the one they'd just met.

Chapter 4

Sarah woke up the next morning feeling like she was on a mission. The more she thought about Jackie, the more certain she was that Jackie's attitude was just a front—a big act. No one could be all that mean and nasty. Okay, maybe Maura Kingsley could be, but she was one of a kind. For some reason, Jackie was determined to make everyone dislike her. Sarah was determined to find out why—and break through that act.

Around the room, the girls were stirring and sitting up, rubbing eyes and yawning.

"Good morning," Sarah called out cheerfully.

A chorus of sleepy "good mornings" came back. Jackie was silent as she got out of bed and stretched. Sarah was about to climb down her ladder when she noticed Erin, lying on the top bed in her bunk. With her eyes half shut, she

43

thrust a leg over the side of the bed. Obviously, she didn't realize she wasn't in her single bed on the floor.

"Erin, watch out!" Sarah yelled.

Startled, Erin leaned forward. Then she grabbed the post and just managed to keep from tumbling down.

"Be careful," Trina exclaimed. And Jackie started laughing. Erin shot her a baleful look, and then, with as much dignity as possible under the circumstances, she climbed down the ladder. With one last withering glance at Jackie, she stalked into the bathroom.

"Did you sleep okay?" Sarah asked Jackie.

Jackie didn't reply. She bent down, and fumbled under her bed, pulling out the same black jeans and shirt she'd worn yesterday.

"I've got a clean Sunnyside tee shirt I can lend you." Sarah pulled it out of the drawer and offered it. "I'd give you shorts too, but they'd probably be too big."

"You can borrow a pair of my shorts," Megan said.

Jackie eyed the shirt scornfully. "I'm not wearing *that*. It's stupid looking."

Trina approached her, smiling. "Jackie, it's your first full day at Sunnyside. We just want you to fit in and feel comfortable."

"Yeah, well, maybe I don't want to fit in." Jackie snatched up her jeans and shirt and headed for the bathroom. She practically collided with Erin who was on her way out. "Excuse *you!*" Erin said. Jackie didn't say a word and disappeared into the bathroom.

Katie, still sitting on her bed, shook her head. "That girl's hopeless."

"We don't know that," Sarah argued. "Maybe she doesn't feel well. Or maybe she's homesick." She turned to Trina. "Like that little Beth."

"She's not homesick," Katie said, climbing down. "She's just mean. Honestly, I think she's meaner than Maura Kingsley."

Megan giggled. "Maybe we should get them together and they could have a meanness contest."

"C'mon, you guys," Sarah persisted. "You promised you'd be nice to her. I think the only way to deal with her is to bombard her with friendship."

"That's right," Trina agreed. "I think that's the way to get through to her."

"I'd like to bombard her, all right," Erin muttered. "But not with friendship."

They were getting dressed when Carolyn came out of her room and surveyed the cabin. "Where's Jackie?" she asked anxiously.

"In the bathroom," Katie said. "Maybe if we're lucky she'll climb out the window and run away."

Carolyn sat on the edge of Trina's bed. "Girls, I know she's not being very nice. But hang in there, okay? It's just for a week."

"Why does she act like that?" Megan asked.

Carolyn studied her fingernails. "Jackie . . . well, she's got some problems. Her parents are very worried about her. They don't know why she's been acting like this. In fact, that's why they sent her here. They hoped she might make some friends and talk to them about what's bothering her. Just try to be kind to her."

I knew it, Sarah thought. There *is* a reason for the way she's acting. But what could it be?

Jackie came out of the bathroom, and the room fell silent. Carolyn got up. "Let's go to breakfast. Isn't this blueberry pancake day?"

It was. Everyone at the dining hall tables was digging in, but Jackie eyed her pancakes with a look of disgust. "I hate blueberries."

"Just eat around them," Megan suggested. But Jackie just put her elbows on the table and rested her chin in her hands. "I'm not hungry."

Sarah tried to start an upbeat conversation. "Hey, arts and crafts is going to be fun today."

46

She turned to Jackie. "We're designing our own sweatshirts."

"How thrilling." Sarcasm dripped from her mouth. That pretty much killed the conversation. When breakfast was over, they headed back to the cabin for cleanup. Everyone was busily making her bed and putting things away when Sarah noticed that Jackie was just sitting on her bed.

The others noticed too. "Aren't you going to make your bed?" Katie asked.

"Why should I? It'll just get messed up again when I go to bed tonight."

Trina explained. "We have inspection every morning. If the beds aren't all made, we get a demerit."

"So what? I don't care if you get a demerit or not." With that, Jackie sauntered out of the cabin. Trina and Sarah went over to her bed and started smoothing the sheets.

"You know what I think?" Megan said. "I'm wondering if this is a test. Remember how Ms. Winkle kept talking about the Sunnyside spirit and how we have to look for the inner qualities in a person? Maybe this is her way of testing us to see how hard we'll try to find those inner qualities."

The other girls shook their heads in amuse-

47

ment. Megan had a very vivid imagination. "Well, if this is a test," Katie said grimly, "it's pretty hard. And I have a feeling I'm going to fail it."

In the arts and crafts cabin, Sarah studied the design for her sweatshirt. She still hadn't been able to come up with anything she could draw to symbolize "science fiction." Donna came over to help.

"What's the problem?"

"I'm just not any good at drawing," Sarah told her.

"Then why bother with drawings? Look, you can just have the words written in different ways all over the sweatshirt." With her finger, Donna demonstrated on a plain white sweatshirt. "See, you could have mystery here, along the shoulder, and romance slanted this way, and science fiction down here. For variety, you could do some words in print, others in script, and some in all capitals."

Sarah started to get excited. "That would look neat! And how about if I had 'read' in big letters across the front?"

"Fantastic!" Donna exclaimed. She glanced around the room. "Jackie, are you sure you don't want a sweatshirt to work on?"

48

Jackie was leaning against the wall, with an expression of total boredom. "No."

Donna continued around the table. "Oh, Katie, this looks wonderful."

Sarah leaned over to see what Katie was doing. Against a blue background, she had dabbed small silver spots. Now she was carefully painting a silver crescent moon. "Wow!" Sarah said. "That's really artistic. Jackie, come see what Katie's done."

Jackie rolled her eyes and looked as if there were a zillion things she'd rather do than look at Katie's sweatshirt. But with a big sigh, she came up behind Katie.

And then something happened. Sarah couldn't tell how or why, but somehow Jackie's elbow knocked the jar of silver paint. And suddenly there were pools and streams of silver running down Katie's sweatshirt.

Katie jumped off her stool. "You creep!" she yelled at Jackie. "You did that on purpose!"

Something about the way Jackie shrank back and the surprise on her face made Sarah jump up too. "Oh no, Katie, it was an accident!"

And Trina joined the defense. "I'm sure Jackie didn't mean to do that!"

But now Jackie appeared to have recovered from the shock. She folded her arms across her chest and stared right back at Katie with a little smirk—as if she *had* done it on purpose. And as if she were proud of it!

Katie caught the expression too. "She did! She meant to ruin it!"

Donna looked upset. "Girls, girls, please!"

Sarah grabbed Trina's arm. "Let's take Jackie outside for a walk."

"Yes, why don't you do that," Donna said, as she dabbed at Katie's messy sweatshirt with a rag.

Sarah was a little surprised at the ease with which Jackie allowed herself to be led outside. "Oh, Jackie," Sarah said, "you didn't really mean to ruin her shirt, did you?"

Jackie stared at the ground and shrugged. "What if I did?"

"But you didn't," Trina insisted. "I saw you. It was an accident. Why are you pretending it wasn't?"

"Oh, leave me alone," Jackie muttered. She turned away from them. Trina and Sarah stared at each other helplessly.

From around the side of the building, a figure appeared. It was Beth, the little homesick camper. "Hi, Beth," Trina said. "How are you?"

If anything, she looked even sadder than before. "I just came from the infirmary," she said.

"I told them I was sick, but the nurse said nothing was wrong with me. I got her to call my parents, though."

"What did they say?" Sarah asked.

Beth was fighting back tears. "They said I had to stay. But I'm going to make them take me home."

"How?" Trina asked.

"I don't know yet. But I'll think of a way." Slowly, she walked away. When Sarah looked back at Jackie, she realized that the black-haired girl had been listening.

"What's the matter with her?" Jackie asked.

It was the first time she'd shown any interest in anything at Sunnyside. "She's homesick," Sarah said. "Worst case I've ever seen." And then an idea struck her. "Jackie, are you homesick? Is that why you hate being here?"

"Homesick? Me? Hah!" And she turned back against the wall.

"Do you miss your parents?" Trina asked.

Jackie turned back toward them. Was that a tear in her eyes? Sarah adjusted her glasses. Yes, that was *definitely* a tear! Was this the answer? Did Jackie miss her parents? Was that why she was acting so awful—so she'd get sent home?

But Jackie's next words took her by surprise.

51

"No, I don't miss them, not one tiny bit. I *wanted* to get away from them! They're stupid!"

With that, she ran off.

Sarah and Trina watched her retreating figure. "Gosh," Sarah whispered. "Do you think she meant that?"

"How could anyone feel like that about her own parents?" Trina asked in wonderment.

Sarah remembered something. "Carolyn said her parents are getting divorced."

"But that wouldn't make her hate them," Trina said. "When my parents got divorced, I felt really sad. But I didn't act like that."

Sarah couldn't even imagine Trina being as nasty as Jackie. But then something else occurred to her. "You know, up to now we've only seen Jackie being mean. But just now, she wasn't mean. She was angry. Maybe that's one of those inner qualities we're supposed to look for."

Trina nodded slowly. "Maybe." But her face was troubled. "I hope we can find more inner qualities. And I hope they're not all like that."

The atmosphere at the dinner table that evening wasn't any better than the atmosphere at breakfast. All day, Jackie had been sullen. Katie and Erin had totally given up on her. And Megan just avoided her.

Only Sarah and Trina had made an effort to drag her to the different activities. And Jackie would never participate.

They all just ate, without talking, and it was very uncomfortable. Sarah was glad when she saw Ms. Winkle go to the front of the room. At least listening to announcements would be better than eating in silence.

"Girls, I'm sorry to report that we have a problem." Ms. Winkle paused to make sure she had everyone's attention.

"Some items have disappeared from two cabins. Now, I can't believe that a Sunnyside girl would steal. Maybe somebody borrowed these things. In any case, I want that person, whoever she is, to bring them to my office. If she does that by tomorrow, I promise she will only receive a demerit as punishment."

A hush fell over the room. At all the tables, girls were looking at Ms. Winkle in disbelief. And then, all at once, everyone was whispering.

Sarah could understand the reaction. As long as she'd been going to Sunnyside, she'd never heard of anyone stealing anything from anyone else.

And an awful thought hit her. She looked at

53

Jackie. She was staring at her barely touched plate. And then Sarah looked at Trina.

Without exchanging a word, she knew they were both thinking the same thing.

Chapter 5

When Ms. Winkle went to the front of the room at breakfast the next morning, she didn't look any happier than she had the evening before. She started off with the usual announcements about activities and trips. And then her voice dropped.

"Girls, the missing items have not been returned. And last night, a third item disappeared from a cabin."

From the back of the room, a camper waved her hand and stood up. "Ms. Winkle, what kinds of things are being stolen?"

Ms. Winkle seemed to wince at the word "stolen." "Well, there's a stuffed animal—I believe it's a teddy bear. And a tennis racket, and last night, a portable cassette player." Her face became very sad. "It gives me great pain to think we might have a thief at Sunnyside. Please, if anyone knows anything about these items, come see me. Whoever you are, I know you're feeling very bad about this. And if you return them, and we have a talk, we'll work it out."

Sarah tried very hard not to look at Jackie. She concentrated on downing the last of her orange juice. Carolyn rose from her chair. "Are you all ready to go back?"

Everyone got up and started out. Sarah lingered in the back of the group and motioned to Trina. "Do you think it was Jackie who took those things?"

"I don't know," Trina said. "Remember what she said about shoplifting with her gang?"

"But I still think that's a big act," Sarah insisted. "Trina, we've just got to get her to talk to us."

"Thank goodness the others didn't hear her say that stuff about shoplifting," Trina said, glancing ahead. "The way Katie and Erin feel about her, they'd probably suspect her immediately." Seeing Jackie walking alone, they hurried to catch up with her.

"Boy, it's really warm today," Sarah said. "Aren't you hot in those jeans?"

Jackie didn't have to reply. The sweat on her brow made the answer obvious. But she actually nodded, and Sarah was encouraged.

"You should go swimming with us," she said. "We have free swim today, no lessons, so it's more fun."

"Did you bring a bathing suit?" Trina asked.

Jackie actually spoke. "Yeah."

Inside the cabin, everyone got to work making beds and straightening up. For a second, Jackie just stood there. Then, to Sarah's surprise and pleasure, she actually started making her bed. Sarah poked Trina, who looked and gave Sarah a thumbs-up sign.

But no one else seemed particularly pleased. Erin glanced down from the top of the ladder. "Gee, it's nice of you to help out for a change," she said sarcastically.

In response, Jackie pounded her pillow. Erin looked unnerved, as if Jackie were going to attack her next.

After inspection, they all changed into their bathing suits and headed for the pool. Katie and Erin walked on ahead. Megan seemed undecided whether to hang back with Sarah, Trina, and Jackie or run ahead to join the others. "Stay with us," Sarah urged, and she did, though she didn't say much and she kept peeking at Jackie as if she were afraid of her.

For a moment, they walked in silence. Then

57

Sarah gathered up her courage. "Don't you think it's awful about those missing things?"

"Terrible!" Megan exclaimed. "I can't believe there's a creepy person like that at Sunnyside! It's weird that it just started happening this week. It must be one of the new people who's doing it."

Sarah glanced nervously at Jackie. Trina spoke up quickly. "Yeah, one of those young kids, maybe."

To Sarah's amazement, Jackie joined in the conversation. "It has to be a little kid. Who else would steal a teddy bear? Wait till I tell the gang back home about this. With all the things to steal at this camp, why would anyone bother with a teddy bear?"

Aghast, Megan looked at Jackie. "It's wrong to steal *anything!*"

Sarah waited apprehensively. To her relief, Jackie didn't start bragging about her shoplifting.

Since it was free swim day, the pool was filled with splashing campers playing and just generally fooling around. Every time a girl got out, someone pushed her back in, so there was a lot of yelling and laughing.

Along the side, girls from cabin nine just sat on the ledge, delicately slapping the water with their feet. They never went in the water on free swim days, because they didn't want to get their hair wet.

Sarah, Trina, and Megan jumped in. Then Sarah watched in awe as Jackie executed a graceful dive.

"Wow," Sarah said when Jackie returned. "I wish I could do a dive like that."

"It's easy," Jackie said.

"Really? Will you show me how to do it?"

Jackie looked torn. She seemed on the verge of making one of her smart-aleck retorts, but at the same time, Sarah could tell she was pleased to be asked.

"Okay," she said finally. "Get out of the pool."

Sarah did, and they stood side by side on the ledge. "First, you lean forward, like this," Jackie began, but she was interrupted.

"Oh no, watch out everyone!" Maura called to the others sitting on the ledge. "Sarah's going to dive! Get back or we'll all get splashed."

Sarah could feel her face turning red. She'd lost weight that summer, and she knew she wasn't as chubby as she'd been when she first got to camp. But she was still very sensitive to those nasty cracks Maura always made about her weight.

And she always said them loud enough for

everyone to hear. Katie swam over to the ledge. "Don't let her bother you," she said to Sarah.

"Who is she?" Jackie asked.

Megan hopped up on the ledge. "Maura Kingsley. She's the meanest girl at Sunnyside." She dived back into the pool and started swimming.

"Or maybe second meanest, now," Katie muttered, and swam away.

Luckily, Jackie didn't hear her. She was eyeing Maura thoughtfully. Then she turned back to Sarah. "Then, put your arms over your head—"

But again, Maura interrupted. "Are you going to swim, too, Sarah? Because maybe we should warn everyone that there's going to be huge waves in the pool. Hey, maybe we ought to get some surfboards!"

The other cabin nine girls sitting around started laughing hysterically. Sarah knew she was on the verge of tears, and she tried desperately to hold them back.

Jackie moved over to Maura and faced her. Sarah watched in dismay. Had Jackie just recognized a soulmate? Was she going to join in the taunts?

But Jackie's voice was oddly sweet. "Are you going to dive in?"

"No," Maura said. "I don't want to get my

hair wet." She patted her immaculate hairstyle. "Some of us care how we look." She eyed Jackie's spikey hair with a sneer.

"Oh, too bad," Jackie said. "I could use a good laugh."

Maura tossed her head. "I happen to be a very fine diver. And by the way, you did that swan dive all wrong."

Jackie's eyes widened and she looked positively shocked. "Really? What was I doing wrong?"

"You didn't have your feet together. And your back wasn't arched properly."

Jackie nodded seriously. "Oh my, I didn't realize that. Could you show me how to stand the right way?"

Maura got up and stood at the ledge. "You have to keep your feet close together and lean like this, and—"

She didn't get any further. With one light nudge, Jackie sent her flying out, and she landed in the water with a splashy belly flop.

Sarah clapped her hand over her mouth, but she was laughing so hard she couldn't keep it there. Even Trina, who usually didn't approve of such things, was giggling.

When Maura emerged from the water, it was very obvious that she didn't find any humor in the situation at all. She climbed out of the pool and screamed for the swimming coach. "Darrell! That girl pushed me in! I could have drowned!"

The handsome counselor hurried over with a look of annoyance on his face. "What's going on here?"

"Oh, Darrell, everyone pushes each other in," Sarah said. "It's no big deal. She's just making a fuss."

But Maura was still yelling and screaming, and now all the other cabin nine girls had joined in accusing Jackie. Sarah could tell that Darrell was getting even more irritated.

"I've told you girls I don't want any horsing around during free swim," he said.

"Send her back to her cabin!" Maura shouted.

With alarm, Sarah noticed that Jackie was getting that now-familiar hostile expression. She could tell that any minute now Jackie would say something that could get her in real trouble. "Don't worry," Sarah said quickly. "We're leaving." She grabbed Jackie's arm. Trina got up too, and the three of them hurriedly left the pool area.

"Thanks for standing up for me," Sarah said gratefully. "I really appreciated that."

"I didn't do it for you," Jackie said coldly. "She was just getting on my nerves."

But Sarah didn't believe that. She had a tingly feeling that she had just witnessed one of Jackie's inner qualities. "Did you see that look on her face when she went in?"

"And did you see her hair when she got out?" Trina asked, giggling. The memory of Maura's fury made Sarah start giggling too. And the giggles were catching. Even Jackie finally cracked up.

The girls collapsed on the ground, still laughing. "See?" Sarah said between giggles. "We *do* have fun here at Sunnyside!"

"I guess," Jackie said reluctantly. Her giggles had ended abruptly. "At least it's better than being at home."

Sarah and Trina stopped laughing. "Jackie," Trina said tentatively, "why are you so mad at your parents?"

Sarah half expected Jackie to come back with something like "none of your business." But she didn't. She plucked at a piece of grass and carefully split it down the middle. Then she spoke. "They're getting divorced."

Even though they already knew that, Sarah and Trina acted as if they hadn't. "That's too bad," Sarah said sympathetically.

Jackie gave her a sidelong look. "I don't suppose you could understand what that means. I'm sure you have a perfectly happy home with your mom and dad, right?"

"Just with my dad and my sister," Sarah said. "My mother died when I was little."

Jackie seemed startled. Then she turned to Trina. "Well, I guess you come from one of those homes like on television shows. I'll bet you've got a big happy family."

Trina shook her head. "We're happy, but it's just me and my mom. My parents are divorced."

Jackie was totally unprepared for this news. She stared at Trina in total astonishment. "When—when did they get divorced?"

"Just a few months ago," Trina replied calmly.

Jackie shook her head in disbelief. "But . . . you act so happy."

"I *am* happy," Trina said. "I mean, I was sad when they got divorced. But now I know it was the best thing for them to do."

"Best for *them*, maybe," Jackie muttered. "But what about for you?"

Trina smiled slightly. "I was pretty depressed for a while. I didn't want to see any of my friends. But after a while, I realized it was going to be okay. When they were married, they argued a lot, and that was yucky. Now my mom seems a lot happier. And I see my dad every weekend. He acts happier too. So it's actually better for me too."

Jackie was silent for a minute. "I'm so angry at them!" she burst out suddenly. "How could they do this to me?"

"They're not doing anything to you—" Trina started to say, but Jackie wouldn't let her finish.

"Yes, they are! And I'm getting back at them for it." She said this with a strange sort of satisfaction.

"How?" Sarah asked.

Jackie's mouth was set in a grim smile. "I'm not speaking to them. And I go out every night and I don't tell them where I'm going."

"Where do you go?" Trina asked.

For a moment, Jackie didn't answer. Then she actually appeared to be a little embarrassed. "To the library or a book store. I just sit in there and read. But I don't tell them that. I let them think I'm hanging around on the streets."

"With your gang," Sarah finished.

Jackie nodded.

"But you're not really in a gang," Sarah continued.

Jackie's mouth opened, and she looked like

she was about to argue. Then she closed her mouth and gave an abashed grin. "No, I made all that up."

"And the part about the shoplifting too?" Trina asked. Jackie nodded.

Sarah and Trina looked at each other and smiled in relief. Sarah felt a thrill of triumph shoot through her. She'd been right! It was all an act. Now everything could be normal. Jackie would stop acting so mean, she'd join in the activities, and the other kids in the cabin would like her.

But then Jackie picked up a rock. And she tossed it with a force that told them she was still feeling angry.

"You know," Sarah said casually, "I don't remember when my mother died. I was only three. But my father said that after she died, my personality changed for a while. All of a sudden I started throwing tantrums all the time, fussing about everything, refusing to go to sleep, all that stuff. He said I was the angriest child he'd ever seen."

Jackie looked at her curiously. "Why were you acting like that?"

"I don't know," Sarah said honestly. "Like I said, I don't even remember this. But my dad talked to a doctor. And the doctor said I was angry because I felt deserted, like my mother left me on purpose and I blamed her. I felt like it was all her fault."

"But it wasn't her fault," Jackie said.

"Of course not! But that was how I felt. What I'm saying is, I guess it's natural to feel angry when anything changes in your family."

Jackie sniffed. "Well, I'm not three years old."

"Exactly!" Trina said. "But you're acting like you are."

Sarah couldn't believe Trina had just said that. Here they'd finally gotten Jackie to open up to them, and now Trina was insulting her! And Trina was *never* rude! Why did she say that? She looked at Jackie, worried, waiting to see how she was going to take this.

But Jackie didn't jump up and storm off. Instead, she just looked at Trina for a long time. And then, to Sarah's astonishment, she actually smiled—a real smile.

"Yeah. I guess I am."

Trina put an arm around Jackie's shoulder. "It's okay to feel angry. But you have to understand that this is their decision, and they're not doing it to hurt you. They're doing it to make all your lives better."

Sarah gazed at Trina in admiration. She could be so wise sometimes.

"I've made a mess of things here, haven't I?" Jackie lowered her head. "I know Katie and Erin hate me. And I don't think Megan's too crazy about me either."

Neither Trina nor Sarah bothered to deny this. "Well, you've still got five whole days here," Sarah said optimistically. "There's still time to show everyone the real you. And I know they'll start liking you."

Trina hopped up. "It's almost time for archery. Let's go back to the cabin and change."

Sarah made a face as she got up. "Archery. Yuck. I can never hit the target," she told Jackie. "Are you any good at archery?"

"I don't know," Jackie admitted. They started toward the cabin. "I've never tried it. But I've got pretty good aim." She picked up another rock. "See that tree stump over there?" She threw the rock. It hit the top of the stump.

"Amazing," Sarah said. "You're going to be great at archery. Your aim is perfect!"

"Mmm," said Jackie thoughtfully. And she looked at them with twinkling eyes. "Will Maura be there?"

Laughing, the three of them put their arms around each other and ran to the cabin. Quickly they changed, and this time Jackie accepted

68

Sarah's offer of a Sunnyside tee shirt and a pair of Trina's shorts.

Then they headed for the archery range. As they passed the woods, Jackie asked, "What's in there?"

"Just woods," Sarah said. "We go hiking there sometimes and on nature walks."

Jackie gazed at the cool, quiet darkness wistfully. "I'll bet the woods would be a nice place to hide and just be by yourself."

"Don't try it," Trina warned her. "There are strict rules about the woods. You're never supposed to go in there without a counselor."

The others were already at the archery range, stringing their bows and lining up in front of targets. Jackie suddenly seemed reluctant to join them. "I—I feel funny about this. I don't know what to say to everyone."

"You don't have to say anything right now," Trina said reassuringly. "Look, why don't I take you over and introduce you to the counselor." They took off, and Sarah waved to Katie and the others. Then she joined them in line.

"Where have you been?" Megan asked.

"Trina and I were talking to Jackie."

"How can you stand being around that girl?" Erin demanded.

"Oh, she's not so bad," Sarah said. "Did you

69

see what she did to Maura, pushing her in the pool? Wasn't that neat?"

"She'd do that to anyone," Katie said. "She's mean enough to push one of *us* in the water. It was just luck that she happened to pick Maura."

"That's not true," Sarah said. "Maura was picking on me, as usual. That's why Jackie did it. She was just getting back at her for me."

Erin shook her head. "Oh, Sarah, you're such a softie. You like *everyone.*"

She made that sound like a major personality flaw. "But Jackie's really okay," Sarah insisted. "Trina and I just had this long talk with her. That was just a big act she was putting on, because she was angry about her parents getting divorced. She's actually a nice person."

Megan looked doubtful. "I don't think nice people hang out in gangs."

"But that was all a lie," Sarah said eagerly. "All that stuff about gangs and shoplifting and—" she stopped and gasped. What had she just said? Oh, if only she could swallow her words!

But it was too late. Katie, Erin, and Megan all had the same expression on their faces.

"Shoplifting," Katie breathed. "Stealing things from stores, huh?"

"It was a lie," Sarah insisted fervently. "She was just putting on a big, mean, tough act!"

"Oh, sure," Erin scoffed. "Personally, she seems like a real criminal type to me."

Katie nodded in agreement. Her face was grim. "Well, if she shoplifts, that means she's a thief. And if she'd steal stuff from stores, what's going to stop her from stealing things other places?"

"Like here," Megan murmured.

Katie nodded. She turned to where Trina had taken Jackie, and fixed a stern glare on the new girl.

"You know what, guys? I think we can be pretty sure who's been swiping things at Sunnyside."

Chapter 6

Oh, *why* had she opened her big mouth, Sarah wondered miserably as she curled up on her bed. It was rest period, and she had her book open and propped on her stomach. But for once, she couldn't focus on reading. She was too worried and too angry at herself. She'd wanted so much to help Jackie. And instead, she'd made everything worse for her. Now they all thought Jackie was the camp thief.

She peeked over the top of the book to see what the others were doing. Trina was actually taking a nap. Erin was painting her nails again. Below her, Sarah was reasonably sure that Megan was daydreaming. And Katie was acting restless. She had climbed down from her bed and was rummaging through her drawers.

Everyone seemed to be acting normally. Maybe they'd forgotten what she'd said about

Jackie and the shoplifting, Sarah thought hopefully.

As usual, Katie broke the required silence. "Has anyone seen my cassette player?" she demanded.

"No," Megan said, and Sarah shook her head. Katie slammed the drawer shut and faced the others. "It's missing."

Sarah gasped. "Oh no! You think the thief came in here?"

Katie put her hands on her hips. "I think the thief *lives* here."

Erin's hand holding the polish brush froze in midair. "Where *is* Jackie, anyway?"

"Probably hiding my cassette player somewhere," Katie replied.

"She is *not,*" Sarah said hotly. "I happen to know that she's visiting Ms. Winkle." She wished Trina would wake up and help her defend Jackie.

Below her, Megan was apparently not as lost in her daydreams as usual. "Gosh," she said, "imagine what Ms. Winkle will say when she finds out her own niece is the thief."

Sarah slammed the book shut and scrambled down the ladder. "Megan, do *you* think Jackie's the thief too?"

Megan shrugged. "Well, you said that she

74

said she shoplifts back home. And all the stealing started right after she came."

"But that's just a coincidence," Sarah began, but she couldn't get any further. The cabin door opened and Jackie came in. She must have known she'd been the object of discussion, because everyone was looking at her.

"How was your visit?" Sarah asked quickly, but at the same time, Katie said, "We're looking for my cassette player. Any idea where it might be?"

The tone of her voice implied that she was sure Jackie knew where it was. Sarah watched Jackie's face carefully, trying to read her expression.

At first, Jackie seemed taken aback. Then her face took on that hostile, surly look. "No." She started for her bed, but stopped as she passed Katie's. "Isn't that it?"

Sarah hadn't noticed the thin strap hanging down from Katie's bedpost. Squinting, she could see that the player had become buried under the mattress.

Katie climbed up the ladder and retrieved the cassette player. Sarah looked up at her meaningfully. Katie really should apologize for talking to Jackie like that, she thought. Of course, she hadn't actually come right out and accused

Jackie of stealing it, but she sounded like she had.

Katie didn't say a word, though. She put the headphones on and hit a button on the player. Then she pulled it off. "Darn. I forgot I don't have batteries."

Jackie stared at her coldly. "Well, *I* didn't steal your batteries." Then she sat on her own bed.

The tension in the cabin was unbearable. Sarah tried to think of a way to break it. "Um, Jackie, you said you hang out in the library a lot back home. You must like reading."

"Yeah."

"Do you want a book? I've got some good ones under the bed."

"No." There was a pause, and then she added, "thanks. But I just feel like resting." She closed her eyes.

Sarah climbed back up to her bed and returned to her book. But she couldn't concentrate. It was all her fault that Katie was so suspicious of Jackie. If only she hadn't let it slip about the shoplifting! How was she going to prove that Jackie wasn't what she seemed? Why couldn't Jackie open up to all of them the way she had to Sarah and Trina? They'd see she couldn't be the camp thief!

Trina woke up, and yawned. "Gosh, I actually fell asleep. Anything exciting happening?"

Before anyone could respond, Carolyn came out of her room. "Time for arts and crafts," she announced.

"I just hope Donna has another sweatshirt for me," Katie said loudly, "because my first one was ruined." She looked pointedly at Jackie. Sarah held her breath as Jackie faced Katie.

"It was an accident," Jackie said. "And I'm sorry."

Katie looked a little taken aback by the unexpected apology. But she recovered quickly. "Sure it was." And she marched out of the cabin.

"She really doesn't like me," Jackie said to Sarah and Trina as they walked to the arts and crafts cabin. "I guess I can't blame her."

"She'll come around," Trina promised. "Katie doesn't hold grudges forever."

"Offer to help her fix her sweatshirt," Sarah suggested. But that turned out not to be necessary. Somehow, Donna had managed to clean off the silver paint that had spilled on Katie's shirt. Everyone got to work on her design, and for a while there was peace.

"Finished!" Katie cried out. "Look, everyone!" She held up her sweatshirt.

"Katie, that's beautiful!" Sarah exclaimed. It really was. Katie had created a magical-looking night sky, full of moons and stars on a dark blue background. Everyone oohed and ahhed over it.

Katie laid it carefully on the table to dry, and then walked around the table examining everyone else's work. "That's cool," she said, peeking over Sarah's shoulder.

Sarah had to admit her sweatshirt was interesting. Along with mystery, romance, and science fiction, she had drama, poetry, suspense, and western—even though she didn't like cowboy books at all. Down one sleeve she'd written horror; the other sleeve read humor. She'd left a big empty space in the center of the shirt.

"What are you going to put there?" Katie asked.

"It's going to say 'read,' " Sarah told her. "What color do you think I should use?"

When Katie didn't reply immediately, she looked over her shoulder at her. Katie's eyes had narrowed, and she wasn't looking at Sarah's sweatshirt. Her eyes were fixed on Jackie.

Jackie had picked up Katie's sweatshirt.

"Hey! That's mine! Put it down!"

"I was just admiring it," Jackie protested.

"Oh, yeah, right," Katie muttered. And to Sarah, she said, "She was probably going to run off with it when I wasn't looking." Her voice was just loud enough for Jackie to hear.

Jackie dropped the sweatshirt. "Why would I want to run off with a stupid sweatshirt?"

Katie snickered. "Yeah, I guess a sweatshirt would be beneath you."

Jackie looked at her in bewilderment. Just then, Donna clapped her hands. "Time to clean up, girls. If you're not done, you can finish tomorrow."

"What do we do now?" Jackie asked Sarah.

"Well, it's free period," Sarah said. "I'm going to ask Donna if I can finish this sweatshirt now. Then I wanted to go back to the cabin and finish my book."

"Megan and I are going riding," Trina said. "Want to come?"

"Okay," Jackie said.

Trina turned to Katie. "You're coming riding with us, aren't you?"

Sarah was surprised when Katie shook her head. Katie never gave up a chance to be with the horses.

"No, Erin and I have something to do." She shot a significant look at Erin, who nodded.

Sarah got permission to finish up her sweatshirt, so she stayed while everyone took off, and another group of campers came into the cabin.

It didn't take her very long to letter the word "read," and paint it in red. Then she headed back to the cabin.

It was a beautiful, sunny day, and she assumed everyone would be outside enjoying it. She was the only camper who preferred to stay inside and read on a day like this. So she was startled to find Katie and Erin in the cabin.

And she was astonished to see what they were doing. Katie was under Jackie's bed, poking around. Erin had Jackie's suitcase open, and she was rummaging through it.

"What are you guys doing?" Sarah asked.

"Looking for the missing stuff," Katie called over her shoulder. "The teddy bear and the cassette player and—what was the other thing?"

"A tennis racket," Erin said. "Katie, check under her mattress."

Sarah was outraged. "I can't believe you guys! You've got no business going through her stuff like this!"

"Sarah, you're the one who said she shoplifts," Katie reminded her.

"But I *told* you it was just an act! She was making all that stuff up, just to shock us. She told Trina and me it was a lie. She's upset about her parents' divorce, and she's been acting weird

80

just to get back at them. If you guys would just give her a break, get to know her—"

"No, thanks," Erin said. "Look, Sarah, she probably said it was a lie because she knows we suspect her."

Sarah sighed heavily and plopped down on Megan's bed. "I'll bet you haven't found anything."

Erin slammed a drawer shut. "No. Katie, did you?"

Katie pulled herself out from under the bed. "No. But I guess she's not so dumb that she'd stash the loot here. It's probably hidden somewhere on the campgrounds. But I'll check under the mattress anyway."

"They're going to be back pretty soon," Sarah warned her. "It's almost time for dinner."

Katie stuck her arm under Jackie's mattress and started feeling around. "I hope she didn't take Starfire riding. Although I guess it would be pretty hard to steal a horse. Hey, there's something under here!"

She pulled out a plain book and opened it. "It's a diary! Maybe she wrote where she put the stuff she stole!"

"Don't you dare read her private diary!" Sarah yelled. "Put it back!"

"Sarah, you better not try to cover up for her,"

Erin said. "You could be considered a—a what-chamacallit to the crime."

"Accessory," Sarah filled in. "But I'm not, because Jackie's not a criminal." She glanced out the window. "Here they come now."

Hastily, Katie shoved the diary back under the mattress. "We'll read it later," she told Erin.

Sarah shook her head wearily. They weren't going to give up, no matter what she said. If only the real thief could be found!

Trina, Megan, and Jackie entered the cabin. "How was your ride?" Sarah asked, hoping Jackie wouldn't notice the furtive looks Katie and Erin were giving her.

"It was fun," Jackie said. "I was a little nervous at first. We don't see many horses in New York. Just the ones pulling carriages in Central Park. And sometimes I see police on horses."

"I guess you stay away from those," Katie said casually.

Jackie gave her a puzzled glance. Then turned back to Sarah. "Anyway, I haven't been on horses much. But Starfire was real gentle—"

"You rode Starfire!" The outrage was clear in Katie's voice. "That's the horse *I* ride!"

"Well, she doesn't belong to you, does she?" Jackie snapped.

"No. And she doesn't belong to you either. I hope you remember that!"

Jackie looked thoroughly confused. Then she shrugged. "I'm going to take a shower before dinner," she said. She put a hand on her wrist, and groaned. "Oh no! I left my watch in the stable. I better run back and get it before someone swipes it."

"Oh, I don't think you need to worry about that," Erin called as Jackie ran out of the cabin.

"What's going on?" Trina said, eyeing Erin and Katie curiously. "Why are you guys talking to Jackie like that?"

Sarah spoke for them. "They think Jackie's the one who's been stealing things."

"Well, you're the one who put the idea in our heads," Erin retorted.

"But how did—oh, Sarah." Trina shook her head reproachfully. "Did you tell them about her bragging?"

"It slipped out," Sarah confessed. "But I told them it was all a big lie! And they don't believe me."

Trina put her hands on the hips and faced Erin and Katie squarely. "Jackie is *not* a thief. She's just a very unhappy girl who's angry at her parents. She was putting on this tough act with them at home to get back at them. If you

83

give her half a chance you'd see she's really not like that at all."

"Look at the facts," Katie argued. "First, she brags about shoplifting. Then things start disappearing at camp. And if she admits she was lying about shoplifting, how do you know she's not lying now when she says she made it up? A liar's a liar as far as I'm concerned."

"I think we should go to Ms. Winkle and tell her we think Jackie's the thief," Erin stated.

"You're going to tell her you suspect her niece?" Megan asked in amazement. "She'll never believe you."

"Besides, you have no evidence," Sarah said. "You can't go around accusing people of things just because you don't like them. You have to have proof."

Katie and Erin looked at each other. Then Katie shrugged her shoulders. "Yeah, I guess we'll have to wait until we actually catch her with one of the missing things."

"Which you won't," Trina said firmly.

Erin tossed her head. "Oh yeah? I wouldn't count on that." She picked up a brush and pulled it vigorously through her hair. "I have a pretty good feeling we're going to find some evidence very soon."

Chapter 7

Sarah watched anxiously as Ms. Winkle got up to make announcements at dinner. But at least she started off with good news. "There will be a movie by the lake tonight right after dinner."

A general cheer went up from the campers. Ms. Winkle let it die down before continuing. "Tomorrow night, we'll be having our first dress-up dinner of the summer. And I've invited the boys of Camp Eagle to join us."

The cheer that greeted this announcement was louder and lasted longer. Ms. Winkle had to hold up her hand to get them quiet. And then her face grew serious. "I'm very distressed to have to tell you we've had a report of a missing watch from one of the cabins. Girls, this has become a very serious problem. We cannot allow this activity to continue here at camp. I'd like to ask all the counselors to meet with me now at my table to discuss this."

Carolyn got up. "Excuse me, girls," she said, and left for Ms. Winkle's table.

"What did she say was stolen?" Erin asked loudly. "A watch?" She looked pointedly at the gold band that rested on Jackie's wrist.

Katie too eyed the watch. "Funny, I don't remember you wearing that when you first came here."

Sarah felt her heart sink as realization dawned on Jackie's face. The dark-haired girl's face became pale. "You think I stole this watch?" she asked.

Erin casually stirred her soup. "Not to mention a few other items."

Jackie looked stunned. "You—you really think I've been stealing all those things at camp."

"Well, here's your chance to prove you haven't," Katie said. "We'll go ask Ms. Winkle which camper had her watch stolen. Then you can show that camper your watch. And we'll see if she can recognize it."

Jackie's mouth fell open, but no words came out.

"Look, if you're innocent, she won't be able to identify it," Katie went on. But she didn't get any further. Jackie stood up, her eyes blazing with fury.

"I don't have to listen to this! I'm going back to the cabin." And she whirled around and marched out of the dining hall.

"That's evidence," Erin said with satisfaction.

"What do you mean?" Sarah said.

"Did you see that guilty look on her face?"

"I wouldn't call it guilty," Trina said. "I'd say she was mad."

"But she refused to show the watch to prove she's innocent," Katie noted. "I'd call *that* suspicious."

"She doesn't have to prove she's innocent," Sarah stated. "A person is innocent until proven guilty. Haven't you ever heard of that?"

Erin smirked. "She looked pretty guilty to me."

"She's angry!" Sarah declared. "And I can't blame her!" She got up. "I'm going to tell her some of us don't think she's a thief."

Trina stood up too. "I'm going with you. Megan, you want to come?"

Megan's eyes darted back and forth. Katie fixed her with a long, hard stare, and Megan seemed to shrivel in her seat. Sarah couldn't really blame her. Katie had a way of intimidating people.

"It's okay, Megan," she said. "You don't have to come with us. We'll meet you guys at the movies."

"If she comes to the movie, I'm not sitting with her," Erin said.

"Me neither," Katie added.

"Sarah and I will sit with her," Trina said quietly. "Megan, you can sit with us if you want. Or with Katie and Erin."

Megan smiled weakly. "How about if I sit half the movie with them and half with you?"

"Poor Megan," Sarah said to Trina as they left the dining hall. "She's sort of caught in the middle. I don't think she really believes Jackie's the thief. But you know how Katie can push people around."

"You're telling me," Trina said fervently, and Sarah grinned. Katie and Trina were best friends. But when Katie was captain of a color war team and Trina was on the other side, Katie tried to make Trina lose games on purpose so her side would win. Katie had a lot of terrific inner qualities though, so the girls just put up with the fact that she tended to be a little bossy.

But this time she was going too far. Sarah

had a feeling that Jackie was really hurt by the accusations.

Sure enough, when they entered the cabin, Jackie was lying face down on her bed. And the pillow was wet.

"Jackie, don't be upset," Trina said, sitting on the bed beside her. "We know you're not the one who's been stealing things. And Katie will realize that as soon as they catch the real thief."

Jackie sat up and wiped her eyes. "She'll probably talk you guys into believing her. By this time tomorrow, you'll all think I'm the thief."

"No way," Sarah stated firmly. "Yeah, I know Katie can be very persuasive, but not this time. Not with us."

Jackie didn't look convinced, but Sarah couldn't think of anything else to say. Well, she thought, actions speak louder than words. "C'mon, let's go to the movies. The three of us will sit together."

Jackie just sat there for a moment. "You know why I didn't want to show my watch?" She pulled it off her wrist. "Look at the inscription."

Sarah and Trina looked closely to read the tiny engraving on the back of the case. It read

"To our darling daughter Jackie, from her loving parents."

"Sometimes, I look at that, and I start crying," Jackie said softly.

Trina reached over and gave her a hug. "I know what you mean."

Jackie put the watch back on and stood up. "Okay. Let's go." They left the cabin together and started down the slope toward the lake. They were about halfway there when Sarah stopped.

"I forgot something."

"What?" Jackie asked.

Sarah grinned. "Sometimes the movie is something really dumb or something I've already seen. So I always bring a book and a flashlight just in case."

"You can go back and get them," Trina said. "We'll wait for you here."

Sarah hurried back up the slope. By the time she got to the cabin, she was out of breath. She pushed the door open and then stopped short. Little Beth, the homesick camper, was standing there.

"Beth! What are you doing here?"

Beth was very pale. "I—I was just . . ."

"Did you come to see me?" Sarah asked. Beth nodded mutely. "We're going to the movie by the lake. You can come and sit with us if you like."

"Okay," Beth whispered. Sarah grabbed her book and her flashlight. Then she led Beth out of the cabin.

"Look who I found," she called brightly to Trina and Jackie.

"Hi, Beth," Trina said. "How's everything going?"

Beth didn't reply. Even with everyone smiling at her, she looked frightened. She reminded Sarah of a scared little kid who'd just been caught raiding the cookie jar.

They reached the lake and joined the crowd waiting for the movie. They picked up sodas and bags of popcorn from the refreshment table, and found a place on the sand.

"I'm glad you haven't left Sunnyside, Beth," Trina said.

"But I will be leaving," Beth said suddenly. "Very soon, I think."

"Oh, are your parents letting you come home?" Jackie asked.

"Not yet," Beth said. "But they will."

Sarah thought she sounded strange, sort of mysterious and secretive. But she had too many other things on her mind right now to think about Beth.

Way over by the water, she could see Katie, Erin, and Megan sitting together. And it saddened her to realize this was the first time they hadn't all sat together for a movie.

Jackie was looking at them too. Sarah put a hand gently on her arm. "Don't worry about them. They'll find out you're not the thief."

"What are you talking about?" Beth asked in her soft, quivering voice.

Trina explained. "Some of our cabin mates think Jackie's the one who's been stealing those things at camp. But we know she's not. Anyway, they've been treating her pretty badly, and Jackie's a little upset."

"Oh."

The movie was starting. Sarah watched for about twenty seconds and then groaned. "I've already seen this."

"I haven't," Trina said.

"Neither have I," Jackie echoed. "Is it any good?"

"Not bad," Sarah said. "Have you seen it, Beth?"

But Beth wasn't there. Sarah figured she must have gone to join her own cabin mates. She settled herself against a large rock, opened her book, and switched on the flashlight.

Actually, she was glad that the movie was one

she'd seen before. She was at the most exciting point in the book. The detective had gathered everyone in the house together, and he was just about to prove who'd poisoned the old man.

She was so caught up in the story, she was only dimly aware of the sound from the film and the laughter in the crowd. She couldn't take her eyes off the pages, and they flew by.

Amazing. The villain turned out to be this quiet, serious student who didn't seem to care about anything but his books and his studies. He wasn't the materialistic type at all, so no one suspected him of poisoning the old man for his money. Only it turned out he didn't have enough money to pay his school tuition, and that's why he did it.

"Find the motive," the detective said, "and you have the criminal. Attending the university was the most important thing in the world to this man. And he felt his studies justified poisoning his uncle."

It's always the one you least suspect, Sarah thought—never the obvious criminal type. She closed the book and looked up at the movie screen.

The movie was almost over. In a way, Sarah was glad, since she didn't have anything else to read. But at the same time, she dreaded the whole group being together in the cabin. If only she could keep Katie and Erin from making those nasty little remarks to Jackie.

Luckily, Erin seemed to have her mind on something else. They were all getting ready for bed, and she was going on about the dress-up dinner tomorrow night.

"I can't *wait* to see Bobby," she squealed.

"Who's Bobby?" Jackie asked Sarah in a whisper.

"Her sort-of boyfriend at Camp Eagle."

"I've got to look fabulous," Erin went on. "Maybe I'll put my hair up in a French braid."

"What are you going to wear?" Megan asked her.

"I can't decide." Erin went to the closet and pulled out two dresses. One was black with a white lace collar, and the other was a flowered print.

"I like the flowered one," Katie said.

Erin examined them both. "Yeah, but with the black dress, I could wear my mother's pearls."

"You brought pearls to camp?" Megan asked.

Erin laughed. "Yeah, it was my mother's bribe to get me to go. This will be the first chance I have to wear them." She went over to the little nightstand by the bunk bed, and

94

opened a drawer. She pulled out a satin box, placed it on the nightstand, and lifted the top of the box.

And then she screamed.

"My pearls! They're gone!"

Chapter 8

Carolyn came flying out of her room. "What's the matter? What happened?"

"My pearls are gone!" Erin wailed. "The ones my mother let me take to camp!"

"Oh, Erin!" Carolyn ran across the room and peered into the box. "Are you sure you couldn't have misplaced them?"

"I haven't taken them out of the box since I got here!" Erin stared into the box, as if she expected the pearls to suddenly reappear. But the box remained empty.

Carolyn shook her head regretfully. "Someone must have come in here while we were at the movie."

"Not necessarily," Katie said. "They could have been stolen anytime in the past few days."

"Or before," Sarah quickly pointed out. "They could have been stolen weeks ago."

"I'm sorry, Erin," Carolyn said. "We'll go see Ms. Winkle in the morning and report this. There's really nothing we can do about it now." She patted Erin's shoulder sympathetically, and went back to her room.

When she left, the cabin was quiet. Erin continued to gaze into the box. Then she turned and faced the others. "There *is* something we can do right now."

"What?" Trina asked.

"We can search this room."

Her words sent a chill through the cabin. "Erin, what are you saying?" Sarah asked in a shaky voice. But Erin didn't need to reply to that. Jackie answered for her.

"She thinks I stole her pearls. And she thinks I hid them somewhere in this cabin."

"Did you?" Katie asked.

Jackie looked at her steadfastly. "No."

"Then I guess you wouldn't mind if we took a look around," Erin said.

"Erin!" Trina exclaimed. "She said she didn't take them. Why can't you just believe her?"

"Because she's lied before," Katie said. "And she just might be lying right now."

Sarah was outraged. "Katie!" But Jackie stopped her from going further.

"Let them search if they want to." And she

98

moved back, away from the bunk. She leaned against the opposite wall, her arms folded across her chest.

Sarah didn't know what to do. Erin and Katie shouldn't be allowed to go through Jackie's things. But she'd seen that determined look on Katie's face before, and she knew there was no stopping her. So she sat down on Megan's bed. Trina and Megan sat on either side of her.

They all watched as Katie looked through Jackie's dresser drawer, picking up things and moving them around. Erin lifted the bed's mattress and peered underneath.

Sarah cast a sidelong glance at Jackie. She was still leaning against the wall, her eyes fixed on Katie and Erin. Her lips were pressed tightly together, and her face was pale.

"There's nothing in here," Katie announced, slamming the drawer shut. "Erin, look under the bed."

"I don't need to," Erin replied. She was feeling under the pillow. "I found them." And, from beneath Jackie's pillow, she pulled out a string of pearls. She held them aloft, and Katie stood alongside her triumphantly.

Sarah's gasp broke the deadly silence that fell on the room. Trina's face was stricken. Megan was the first to speak. "Oh Jackie! How could you?"

Jackie said nothing, and her expression told them nothing either. She just stared at the pearls blankly.

"I'm going to see Ms. Winkle right now," Erin declared.

Jackie still said nothing. Then, abruptly, she pulled away from the wall and walked into the bathroom.

"See?" Katie said. "We were right! She didn't even try to deny it!"

"I can't believe it," Trina murmured.

Neither could Sarah. She felt shocked and dazed. She'd been so sure about Jackie!

"C'mon," Erin said, "let's go see Ms. Winkle."

"But it's after hours," Megan said, glancing furtively at Carolyn's door. "We'll get demerits."

"No we won't," Katie countered. "We'll probably get an award for finding the camp thief. And I think all of us should go together."

Sarah looked at the door leading to the bathroom. Jackie hadn't returned. "What about Jackie?"

"Leave her here," Erin said coldly. "Let her think about how much trouble she's in."

Sarah looked at Trina. "Maybe we should stay here and talk to her."

But Trina shook her head. "I wouldn't know what to say. I still can't believe she deceived us like that. I really thought she was a nice person."

"Me too," Sarah echoed sadly.

Erin placed the pearls in the box, pulled on a jacket, and stuck the box in the pocket. "I'm bringing these with me. I'm not taking any more chances."

Tiptoeing, so Carolyn wouldn't hear them, they left the cabin. And they waited until they were a few yards away before they spoke.

"I wonder where she stashed all the other stuff she stole?" Katie asked.

"Ms. Winkle will make her tell," Erin assured her. "You know, I knew that girl was bad news the first time I saw her. Sometimes you *can* judge a book by its cover."

"She seemed so sincere when she told us about her parents, and how angry she was," Sarah said.

"It was an act," Katie replied. "You thought the way she was behaving when she first got here was an act. Well, now we know that was the *real* Jackie."

Sarah still didn't want to accept that. But

101

she'd seen Erin find the pearls under Jackie's pillow. It was hard and fast evidence. There was no way around it.

The lights were on in Ms. Winkle's cabin, and Katie rapped lightly on the door. They heard Ms. Winkle call "come in," and pushed open the door.

The secretary wasn't there, but Ms. Winkle was at her desk, dialing the telephone. Then she hung up the receiver. "It's still busy," she said.

She was speaking to a figure in the corner, who was sitting there with her head down. When she raised it, Sarah saw that it was Beth. Obviously, she was still trying to get her parents to take her home.

"What are you girls doing here at this hour?" Ms. Winkle asked. Sarah was surprised at how harsh she sounded. She knew they weren't supposed to be out of the cabin without their counselor after nine, but Ms. Winkle seemed more upset than she would have expected.

Katie stepped forward. "It's about all the things that have been stolen at camp. We know who the thief is."

Ms. Winkle rubbed her forehead wearily. "I already know that, girls. Beth just told me the whole story."

But how could Beth know, Sarah wondered.

She turned to look at the younger girl. Her eyes were red, and there was shame written all over her face. And suddenly Sarah understood.

"Beth," she whispered. "You took the stuff?"

Very slowly, she nodded.

"But why?" Sarah asked.

Beth's small voice was tinier than usual. "I wanted to go home. I figured somebody would catch me sooner or later. And I'd be sent home."

Ms. Winkle shook her head sorrowfully. "Oh, Beth. Why didn't you come and talk to me about this? We thought you were just a little home-sick. We didn't realize you wanted to go home that badly."

Beth sniffled, and blew her nose in a tissue. "I didn't think anyone would listen to me. So I just kept sneaking into cabins and taking things. And I waited to get caught."

"Wait a minute," Sarah said suddenly. "Is that why you were in our cabin this evening?"

Beth nodded. "I found the pearls in the drawer. I was going to take them when I heard you coming. So I stuck them under a pillow."

Sarah was confused. "But you just said you wanted to get caught. Why didn't you let me catch you?"

Beth stared at the floor. "You were so nice to

103

me. I didn't want you to be the one to find out I was the thief."

"Beth has returned all the items," Ms. Winkle said. "I'm trying to reach her parents now. Now, you girls get back to your cabin immediately."

The cabin six girls started out of the cabin. Sarah paused at the door. "Bye, Beth. I hope everything's going to be okay." The young girl offered a very small smile and a whispered, "thanks." Sarah joined the others outside.

Trina was in the process of scolding Katie and Erin. "See what happens when you jump to conclusions? You owe Jackie a big apology. Actually, we all do."

At least Katie had the good grace to look seriously ashamed. "I feel like a real jerk."

"You should," Sarah said. "And so should you, Erin."

Erin wasn't quite as ready to be sorry. "Well, if Jackie's such a nice person, she shouldn't go around looking like a hoodlum." But even she looked a little embarrassed.

"Hurry up," Trina ordered. "I'm sure Jackie's sitting in that cabin feeling absolutely awful right now."

They ran the rest of the way and were approaching the cabin when Carolyn ran out.

"Where have you been?" she asked frantically. "I just came out of my room to make sure the lights were out and you were all gone!"

"We just went to tell Ms. Winkle about Erin's pearls," Megan began.

"You know you're not supposed to leave the cabin at night," Carolyn scolded them. "This is going to mean five demerits!" And then she frowned. "Where's Jackie?"

"Isn't she here?" Sarah asked. "When we left, she was in the bathroom."

Carolyn hurried back inside, and the girls followed her. The counselor checked in the bathroom. "She's not here."

"Hey, there's a note on her bed." Trina picked up the sheet of notebook paper. Her eyes widened as she read aloud. " 'I didn't steal those pearls or anything else. But I know none of you will believe me. So I'm leaving. Good-bye.' "

"Ohmigosh," Carolyn breathed. "Girls, we have to find her! Trina, you and Megan come with me, and we'll check the main road. Katie, you and Erin and Sarah get Teddy and have him drive you around the campgrounds."

They all ran out and split up. Sarah had to run fast to keep up with Erin and Katie. They were passing a wooded area when she stopped to catch her breath.

"C'mon, Sarah," Katie yelled.

But Sarah was looking into the dark, gloomy woods. And she suddenly remembered something Jackie had said about them. "That would be a nice place to hide," she'd said. And Sarah called to the others excitedly. "I'll bet she's in there, hiding."

"In the woods?" Erin asked. She shivered. "I'm not going in there to look for her."

"We *can't* go in there," Sarah said. "We've already got five demerits in one day. We'll have to go get Teddy."

Katie was looking thoughtful. "But I could climb that tree there and look out over the woods. Maybe I'll spot her." She went over to the large oak and began climbing it. She hoisted herself up onto one limb, then another.

Sarah was awed. Katie was like a monkey, going higher and higher. She reached up and grabbed a sturdy-looking limb, and pulled herself onto a lower one. And then there was a sickening crack.

Erin screamed. Katie was hanging on to the limb, but her legs were dangling, unable to reach any support. "Help!" she yelled. "I can't move!"

"Get Teddy," Sarah yelled at Erin. But Erin was frozen. All she could do was stand there and scream again. Sarah ran to the tree and looked up. "Jump! I'll catch you!"

"Are you crazy?" Katie yelled down. "We'll both get hurt! You have to get someone to climb up and help me! I can't hold on much longer!"

Sarah debated climbing the tree herself. But she knew that with her short legs, she wouldn't get very far. And Erin was hopeless.

"Hold on!" she yelled. "I'll get Teddy!"

But just then she heard footsteps, running ones, coming toward her from the darkness of the woods. And suddenly, there was Jackie. "What's happened? I heard screaming!"

"Help!" Katie yelled again. Jackie looked up.

Sarah wouldn't have blamed her if Jackie just laughed at Katie and left her hanging there. But she wasn't surprised when Jackie whipped off her jacket. "Hang on! I'm coming!"

Jackie turned out to be as good a tree climber as Katie. She went up the other side, carefully testing each limb before putting her full weight on it. Finally, she was parallel to Katie, and she reached out her arm. Katie grabbed it, and Jackie pulled her to a strong limb.

And within seconds, they were both safe on earth. Katie's hands were scraped from gripping the limb, and Jackie had torn her jeans, but other than that, they were fine.

They all stood there for a moment, giving themselves a chance to calm down. "I guess we should go find Carolyn and the others," Erin said.

Sarah nodded. "I've got something to say first to Jackie." She turned to her. "We know you didn't steal that stuff. That little girl Beth confessed." She paused. "I should have believed you when you said you didn't take the pearls. I'm sorry, Jackie."

Jackie bit her lip. Then she nodded. "Yeah. Okay."

Sarah glared at Erin, who finally spoke. "I'm sorry too, Jackie."

Again, Jackie nodded.

"And I'm really, really sorry," Katie said fervently.

"You should be." Jackie glanced down at her torn pants ruefully. "These were my best jeans."

Chapter 9

"I love dress-up dinners," Erin said. With precise strokes, she applied a rosy gloss to her lips.

"I hate 'em," Katie growled. She was examining the dress her mother had packed for just such occasions. "This dress is so geeky."

"No, it isn't, it's cute," Sarah said, without really looking at it. She was too busy admiring herself in the mirror. The yellow sundress she'd brought for dress-up dinners had been more than a little tight when she'd packed it for camp. Now it fit beautifully.

"Where's Jackie?" Trina asked.

"In the shower," Erin replied. "I wonder what *she's* going to wear." Her tone implied that she didn't expect it to be appropriate.

"Now, Erin," Trina said in a warning voice, "haven't you learned your lesson? You ought to be nice to her from now on. Better than nice."

"Oh, all right." Erin sighed. Just then, Jackie emerged from the shower, wrapped in a bathrobe.

"Gee, you all look nice," she said.

"What are you going to wear?" Megan asked. She was perched uneasily at the edge of her bed, trying not to wrinkle her crisp white linen dress.

"I don't have anything to wear," Jackie said mournfully. "My mother told me to pack a good dress. But I didn't, just to spite her. All I've got are jeans and tee shirts."

Erin went to the closet. She emerged holding her flowered dress. "Would you like to wear this? I think it would fit you." Her voice was casual, but Sarah and Trina gave each other knowing looks. It wasn't like Erin to lend anyone anything. This was her way of saying she was sorry.

Jackie brightened. "Could I? I'd hate to look like a slob when everyone else is dressed up."

Graciously, Erin handed over the dress. "Just don't spill anything on it, okay?"

Jackie slipped on the dress. "This is great! Thanks, Erin."

"Don't mention it," Erin said airily. "I'd offer to do something with your hair, but with that cut, I don't think there's anything that can be done."

Jackie just laughed. "Yeah, it's pretty awful. I used to have really long hair, and my father loved it. That's why I cut it all off." She grimaced. "It seems like everything I did to hurt them only ended up hurting *me.*"

"Jackie," Katie said, "you know that sweatshirt I made in arts and crafts that you liked? I want you to have it."

"Thanks, Katie. But you don't have to give me anything to say you're sorry." She sank on a bed.

"Hey!" Erin yelled. "Don't wrinkle the dress!"

Jackie leaped up, smoothed the back of the dress, and carefully sat down again. "Listen, you guys. I know you're all sorry for thinking I was a thief. And it's partly my fault for acting like such a jerk. So I'm sorry, too."

"And you've still got half a week here," Sarah pointed out. "We can start having some real fun."

"We've got the softball game Friday," Katie reminded them.

Sarah made a face. "That's not exactly what I call fun."

But Jackie looked pleased. "I love softball."

"And you've got great aim," Trina said. "I'll bet you'd make a good pitcher."

"Wait a minute!" Katie protested. "That's my

111

position!" Then she caught a look from Trina, and breathed a resigned sigh. "But I'll let Jackie pitch on Friday."

"Thanks!" Jackie said. Sarah wondered if she had any idea what a big sacrifice that was on Katie's part.

Carolyn came out of her room, and clapped her hands. "You girls look lovely!"

"You don't look half bad yourself," Megan returned. Their counselor was wearing a bright red tank dress that was positively sexy.

"I guess the counselors from Camp Eagle are going to be here tonight too," Erin said knowingly.

Carolyn eyed her innocently. "Erin, don't you think I'd dress up just for you guys?"

"No way," the girls yelled in unison, and Carolyn laughed.

"We understand," Erin said. "I've seen some of those counselors at Eagle, and they're cute." She patted the elaborate French braid on the back of her head. "Of course, I only have eyes for one person. Can we go a little late so I can make an entrance?"

"Sorry," Carolyn said cheerfully. "We're going right now. But maybe you can leave when Bobby gets there and come back in again!"

"That's weird," Jackie whispered to Sarah as

they left the cabin. "If he's her boyfriend, and he's going to be there, why would she want to be late?"

"That's just Erin," Sarah said. "She likes those flirty games. She thinks it's important to play hard-to-get."

"Not me!" Jackie laughed. "If I met a boy I liked, I'd probably come right out and tell him."

"Well, you'll have a lot to choose from tonight," Sarah told her. Sure enough, there must have been at least fifty boys from Camp Eagle hanging out in front of the dining hall. Tables had been set up with punch bowls, and finger foods, and things on crackers.

"Ooh, I see Bobby," Erin said. "But I want him to see me first."

Katie waved to Justin, the boy she'd worked on making dollhouse furniture with. And then Sarah spotted Patrick, who had given her some swimming lessons. But before any of them could talk to the boys, Ms. Winkle came toward them.

Her smile broadened when she saw her niece. "Jackie, you look so nice!"

"Erin loaned me the dress," Jackie told her.

"Erin, that was very nice of you," Ms. Winkle said, and Erin preened. "I'm so glad you girls are getting along so well." Sarah had to cover her mouth to hide her grin. As usual, the camp

113

director had absolutely no idea what really went on at Sunnyside!

"Maybe we can talk Jackie into staying an extra week," Ms. Winkle added.

Erin's face fell. "Don't worry," Jackie told her. "If I stay, I'll take the top bunk."

"Did Beth go home?" Sarah asked Ms. Winkle.

The camp director's smile faded a little. "Yes. Her parents came for her this morning. Some girls just aren't emotionally ready for sleep-over camp, and I'm afraid Beth is one of them. Excuse me, girls, while I go greet some of our guests."

She drifted away, and Sarah turned to Jackie eagerly. "Do you really think you might stay an extra week?"

Jackie cocked her head. "Do you guys want me to?"

"Absolutely," Katie said. "We haven't even been able to get to know each other yet." Megan and Trina agreed, and Erin made a general who cares gesture.

Jackie thought about it. "Okay," she said finally. "I'll stay."

Sarah let out a cheer. "Sshh!" Erin hissed. "Bobby's coming this way." She arranged herself so she'd be looking in the opposite direction.

Katie rolled her eyes in disgust. "I don't want to stick around for this." She ran off to find Justin, and Trina and Megan took off too.

"You guys stay here," Erin begged Sarah and Jackie. "I have to look like I'm talking to someone. I don't want him to think I'm just standing here waiting for him."

"Hey."

At the sound of the male voice, Erin whirled around with a look of exaggerated surprise. "Bobby! What are you doing here?"

Bobby looked around in confusion. "Uh, we were invited."

"Oh, of course! That's right. I'd forgotten!"

How could anyone fall for such a terrible performance, Sarah wondered. "Hi, I'm Sarah," she said to Bobby. "This is Jackie. She's visiting from New York."

Bobby's eyebrows shot up. "New York City?"

Jackie nodded.

"Wow, that's so cool," Bobby exclaimed. "I've never even been to New York. Do you ride on the subways?"

"Sure," Jackie said. "All the time. They're not as dangerous as people think."

"Have you ever been to that museum where they have all the dinosaurs?" Bobby asked.

"The Museum of Natural History? Sure, I've

been there lots of times. It's really neat. They've got this huge room filled with dinosaur skeletons, and they're humongous!"

"I'm really into dinosaurs," Bobby said. "Do they have a tyrannosaurus or a pterodactyl?"

As he spoke, he turned so he was facing Jackie directly—which put his back to Erin. Erin watched them in dismay. Then she pulled Sarah aside.

"Who does she think she is!" she whispered in annoyance. "That little thief!"

"Now, come on, Erin," Sarah admonished her. "You can't call her that. You know she's not a thief."

"Okay, okay, maybe she doesn't steal *things.*" Erin's voice was glum as she observed Jackie and Bobby talking. "But now I'm wondering if she steals boyfriends."

Sarah grinned. And it took lots of willpower not to tell Erin that it would serve her right if Jackie did!

MEET THE GIRLS FROM CABIN SIX IN

CAMP SUNNYSIDE FRIENDS

Coming Soon

CAMP SUNNYSIDE FRIENDS #5
LOOKING FOR TROUBLE

75909-8 ($2.50 US/$2.95 Can)

When the older girls at camp ask Erin to join them in some slightly-against-the-rules escapades, she has to choose between appearing cool and being mature.

Don't Miss These Other
Camp Sunnyside Adventures:

(#4) NEW GIRL IN CABIN SIX

75703-6 ($2.50 US/$2.95 Can)

(#3) COLOR WAR! 75702-8 ($2.50 US/$2.95 Can)

(#2) CABIN SIX PLAYS CUPID

75701-X ($2.50 US/$2.95 Can)

(#1) NO BOYS ALLOWED! 75700-1 ($2.50 US/$2.95 Can)

A CAST OF CHARACTERS TO DELIGHT THE HEARTS OF READERS!